Ew! Ew! Except . . . not ew? Except . . . eeewww! He—I—we— *what?*

My first kiss had come out of nowhere.

And it had been with *Camden King*, of all people.

Seriously sketchy.

Seriously hot.

I glanced at the books Camden had given me—Algebra and a Chemistry problem set with a Post-it note that read *$200*. After this, I would be three percent of the way to my $10,000 goal. Great. Awesome. Not nearly fast enough, but it was a start. I'd earn the money, pay the fine, save the restaurant, and save my college fund. No problem.

It was totally doable.

I thought about Camden kissing me and felt my face go red again.

It was just going to be a little more complicated than I'd thought.

she's so money

cherry cheva

HARPER TEEN
An Imprint of HarperCollinsPublishers

HarperTeen is an imprint of HarperCollins Publishers.

She's So Money
Copyright © 2008 by Alloy Entertainment and Watanee Chevapravatdumrong
All rights reserved. Printed in the United States of America.

alloy**entertainment**
Produced by Alloy Entertainment
151 West 26th Street, New York, NY 10001

Library of Congress catalog card number: 2007037432

ISBN 978-0-06-128853-1

Design by Andrea C. Uva

First paperback edition, 2009
14 RRDH 10 9 8 7 6 5 4 3

For my family

chapter one

"Maya! What are you doing?" my mom yelled in Thai from her usual spot up front by the cash register. "Table Five needs water! Clear Table Eight and ask if they want dessert! Your ponytail is falling out! I need the bill for Table Six!" She paused, then beckoned me over to her as she lowered her voice to a whisper. "Look at Table Fourteen. The man keeps wiping his fingers on his sock." I glanced toward one of the tables in the back corner, giggled briefly with my mom at the sight of one of our customers picking apart a chicken wing and then reaching for his ankle instead of his napkin, and then steeled myself to ask her if I could leave work at eight. Half of the kids in my Advanced Placement History class were at a study group session that my best friend, Sarah, was having at her house, and, like any self-respecting seventeen-year-old waitress whose first priority was school, I was desperate to get there for at least part of it.

"Mom?" I asked. She looked up from her accounting book, her ballpoint pen hovering as it paused halfway through scrawling a row of numbers. "Do you think it would be okay if—"

I didn't get to finish, because the phone rang and she turned to pick it up—"Good evening, Pailin Thai Cuisine"— just as a customer started frantically waving at me from across the room. The guy was sitting in my younger brother's section, but Nat had either gone to the kitchen or disappeared into thin air, so I went over and looked at the guy's glass. There were a few dregs of Thai iced coffee still left in it.

"Can I get a refill?" the guy asked.

Nope, I thought to myself. The last time my parents caught me giving free refills on specialty drinks, they yelled at me for half an hour about how I might as well give away entrées, silverware, our Pad Thai recipe, and my virginity.

Of course, I wasn't going to tell the guy that, so instead I smiled cheerfully and fed him the usual line. "I'm sorry, we don't do refills on iced coffee, but if you'd like to order another—"

"Oh, come on," he interrupted, staring up at me expectantly. "Be a pal."

On a day when I was in a good mood, an extremely cute boy might have had a fighting chance. But this guy was old, with a forehead that was more of a *five*head. Maybe even a *six*head, considering his receding hairline.

I summoned up a soothing voice and said as nicely as I could, "I'm sorry. But if you want to order another—"

"Forget it," he snapped. "Two-fifty is overpriced anyway." He glared at me, then looked back down and dug into his half-eaten curried catfish as his wife gave me an embarrassed smile. I smiled back with an expression that I hoped said, "I understand," and not, "Your husband's a douche," then retreated to my own section by the front window. For a moment I stared blankly out through the gauzy white curtains into the darkness, where the late February snow was having trouble deciding whether to melt or refreeze. There were still some long-overdue-to-be-taken-down Christmas lights hanging on the little sidewalk tree in front of the crafts shop across the street, and I watched as a college professor type walked a small dog past our window, weaving in between some cars before disappearing around the corner. I spent a minute wishing I were outside; the restaurant gets so warm when it's crowded, and the chilly night air would have felt good on my face . . . until I remembered that I was still at work, and I snapped back to attention. A cute young couple with a baby was just finishing up at Table Two, and the mom was now beckoning me over.

Oooh, a chance to score a big tip—parents love it when you play with their kids. It wouldn't technically help my wallet, since everything Nat and I make goes straight into our college funds (also known as the Get as Far Away as Possible from Michigan fund, in my case). But a full tip jar might put my mom in a generous mood.

"Aren't you a cutie!" I cooed at the baby, gently tickling her round, pink-clad stomach and admiring her wispy blond curls. She laughed delightedly and clapped her hands. Then she vomited on the table.

You never saw a family leave a restaurant so fast.

Ten minutes later, the ickier-than-usual table cleanup finished and my hands stinging from a vigorous wash and rewash, I was just about ready to take another stab at asking my mom if I could leave early—maybe this time her gung ho attitude about me getting good grades would trump her dinner rush business instinct. I ducked my head through the swinging kitchen door to say hi to my dad, who could barely hear me over the sizzling seafood dish that he and our assistant chef, Krai, were making, not to mention that he could barely see me through his glasses, which were steamed up from the stove. Nonetheless, he waved cheerfully from underneath his ragged University of Michigan baseball cap, the wooden spoon in his battle-scarred cook's hand spattering a smidge of grease into the air from the motion.

Back in the dining room, my mom was on the phone, taking what sounded like a rather lengthy order. No problem. I could wait it out. She hung up the phone. It rang again. *Argh.*

"Hey," I said, poking Nat in the back as he returned

from making the water rounds to our station behind the bar counter. "Quiz me on my history?" We could see the whole dining room from where we were standing, so as long as we kept an eye out while I was studying, we weren't technically slacking off.

"Eh," he said. His hands were wet from the water pitcher, so he dried them off on a stray napkin, then took off his glasses and lazily polished them on his shirt.

"I'll take that as a yes." I handed Nat a stack of index cards I'd stashed in my apron next to the spare chopsticks, and he rolled his eyes and picked up the top one, putting his glasses back on to read it.

"Okay . . . Name three members of the committee that drafted the original Declaration of Independence." Nat lowered the card and looked at me disdainfully. "Dude, I thought you took A.P. History, not retard history."

"Fewer lame jokes, more helping your sister," I snapped. "Okay. Thomas Jefferson, obviously. Ben Franklin. John Ad—" The phone rang, and kept ringing; my mom had left her station to seat a party of six who'd just come in. I ran to answer the call and Nat took off as well, probably to scout the kitchen for mistaken, sent-back orders he could eat. "Hello, Pailin Thai Cuisine," I said into the phone.

"Maya?" said Sarah's voice. I could hear a bunch of people in the background at her house. "Where are you? We're like, halfway done already."

"Oh my God," I said, sighing. "Still at work. My mom won't let me leave." I fussed with the black cotton string of my apron.

"Are you gonna make it? I have to kick people out in an hour." Sarah's gentle voice sounded apologetic, as if it were her fault that I was stuck at the restaurant.

"I don't know. . . . I kinda doubt it at this point. It's pretty busy tonight. . . ." I looked around, hoping that maybe all of our customers had magically vanished. Nope.

"Well, you can totally look at my notes tomorrow morning if you have time before—"

"Great, thank you!" I practically screamed, then continued rapid-fire, "I owe you big time, but I have a call waiting. Gotta go!" The phone was beeping at me, and I hit the flash button. "Hello, Pailin Thai Cuisine . . . Sure, we do takeout, what would you like to—uh-huh. With tofu? Uh-huh . . ." I finished taking the order, eyeing my flashcards the whole time, then realized that Mom had seated those six people who'd just arrived in my section. Damn.

I took their drink orders and picked up my flashcards again, but then the kitchen bell rang twice, signaling that one of my orders was up. By the time I finished carrying out the three bowls of red curry chicken and wondering why all three people at a table would order the same thing, it was time to get orders from the party of six, and by the time I finished that, a guy on the far side of the room was taking his last bite of crispy duck and pushing his plate away. Forget it—studying at work was a lost cause. I headed over to clear the table.

"Save any room for dessert today?" I smiled brilliantly—the way to a twenty-five percent tip from a guy eating by himself is a no-brainer. He looked up at me.

"That depends. Are you on the menu?"

I twirled the end of my long, black, messier-than-usual ponytail and mentally congratulated myself for deliberately shrinking my official Pailin uniform shirt—a simple dark blue three-quarter-sleeve tee with our logo on it—in the wash to make it tighter. "Not today," I said with a smile, and handed him our illustrated dessert card. Now if only I had that much game when I was talking to boys at school. One time I'd tried to trick myself by pretending that I was waitressing, and I'd ended up asking Gavin, the hot foreign exchange student, how spicy he wanted his beef.

Here at work, though, I was on fire. The guy ordered mango sticky rice *and* coconut ice cream, and ten minutes later he threw down a twenty on top of paying the bill, plus a business card with his phone number. I look every bit the jailbait I am—being five feet one inch tall never helps—so the thing with the business card was pretty squicky. The guy was somewhat hot, but at least thirty-five. On the other hand, twenty bucks is twenty bucks.

"Maya! Come here!"

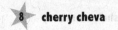

Except, I guess, when your mother's been watching you earn it.

I went over to the cash register, where my mom was glowering. "What did you just do?" She tucked her chin-length hair behind her ears, crossed her arms, and stared at me.

"Uh . . . my job?" I tried to look innocent.

"Your job is *not* to flirt for tips!"

"I wasn't—"

"Yes, you were!" she insisted. "Remember what happened to—"

"Yes, Mom," I interrupted. "You've told me like, a zillion times."

"A zillion plus one!" she declared, launching into her favorite story about this family we know in Ohio. "Annie was a very good Thai girl until she started going out with an American boy. And she started to lie to her parents, and then, one day, her parents came home to find her"—she lowered her voice—"*with* her boyfriend, if you know what I mean."

"I know what you—"

"And so they sent her to live with her aunt in Chiang Mai, where she was free from the corruption of America. She married a nice Thai man and lived a happy, simple life."

"Mom, that's not even true," I said. "They got divorced

and she came back to America and became a travel agent. And you're worrying for nothing, because between school and work, I have no time to date anyway."

"Exactly!" My mom slammed the reservations book shut and banged one of the cash register buttons with a flourish. "School and work, but no boys! You must go to a good college, or else you will also be a travel agent, but in Thailand!"

I had no particular answer to that slice of insanity. She was kind of right, anyway—if I wanted the merit-based scholarship that would enable me to pay for Stanford, assuming I even got in—*fingers crossed, fingers crossed, fingers crossed*—I had to maintain my ridiculously nerdy G.P.A. That left me with basically no time to socialize, but hopefully it would all be worth it.

The order bell was ringing at me again, so I headed back toward the kitchen before she could go on any longer about how even talking to members of the opposite sex leads directly to pregnancy, disease, insanity, death, or all of the above. Of course, avoiding her for the rest of the night wasn't going to work—our restaurant only seats forty-two, unless my parents are in a fire code–breaking mood, and we don't have any booths or screens or anything, so there's literally nowhere to hide. But as long as I didn't piss her off any more, there was still a chance I could get to Sarah's house before her parents booted everyone out.

By nine o'clock we were down to two tables.

"Mom?" I chewed nervously on my pinkie nail for a second. "Is it okay if Nat takes over for the rest of the night so I can go to Sarah's study group? There's almost nobody left here."

She sighed, taking off her reading glasses and putting them down on the credit card reader by the cash register. "Why didn't you study before work?"

"I did, but it's a really important test. *Please*, can I go? I just need to trade notes with some people, and I know if I get just a little extra time I can get an A."

Mom looked at me, her expression unreadable. I mentally crossed my fingers.

"No," she said.

"But—" I started.

"It is not fair to your brother if you leave. Also, it is better for you to study at home with no distractions. At the study group, you just end up chitchatting with your friends." She put her reading glasses back on and turned to her calculator with finality.

I gave up. Time to aim lower on the totem pole. "Hey, Nat, can you take care of my section for the rest of the night so I can study?"

"What, like you're just gonna sit here?" he asked. His hand was wet from the water pitcher again, and he made a move like he was going to dry it off on my shirt.

"Yeah, at the bar," I said, making a face and ducking out of the way.

"Dunno." He shrugged, then smirked and wiped his hand on his apron instead. "What's in it for me?"

"The same deal whenever your next English paper is due," I offered.

"How 'bout you just write it for me?"

"How 'bout I tell your entire class that when you were five, you wore a girl's swimsuit because you wanted to be just like your big sister?"

Nat glared at me and went to check on my section. Finally! I poured myself a Diet Coke and settled onto one of our maroon leather barstools to review the Revolutionary War. I mouthed, "Suck it," at him when a party of eight walked in at nine twenty-five. He smiled politely while flipping me off from behind a menu—there's nothing worse than a bunch of customers walking through the door when you're *this* close to shutting down for the night, especially since my business-savvy parents, terrified of alienating anyone who might become a regular, never rush customers out. Luckily tonight, thanks to my dad's record-fast stir-frying, Annoying: Party of Eight exited after only forty-three minutes. *Phew*. I put down my flashcards and started blowing out the little white votive candles on the tables as Nat practically sprinted to the front of the restaurant and flipped the door sign to CLOSED.

"Hey," Nat said, noticing that I was helping with cleanup. "Study if you want. We made a deal."

"Thanks, but this isn't me being nice so much as it's me trying to get us the hell out of here as quickly as possible." I threw a soapy dish towel at his head and went to the utility closet at the back of the kitchen to get the vacuum cleaner—newly repaired following my recent attempt to suck shrimp tails straight up off the floor so I wouldn't have to touch them—and started vacuuming the dining room floor. The next thing I knew, Nat was shaking my shoulder.

"Dude, you okay?"

I started. "Wha?"

I looked up and realized that I was standing smack in the middle of the dining room, draped over the vacuum cleaner, half-slumped onto the handle.

"You were just staring at the wall like a crazy person."

Huh? Is it possible to fall asleep with your eyes open?

"I'm just tired," I said. He looked at me. "Uh, more than usual," I added.

"Maybe you should start doing speed."

"I will take that into serious lack of consideration," I answered, stretching my arms over my head and jumping up and down a few times to wake up. I kicked the vacuum cleaner and it roared to life as I pushed it with one hand and used the other to punch a button on our espresso machine. Nat walked around wiping tables and pushing chairs out of my way whenever I needed to vacuum under them, as my mom lovingly dusted our restaurant's good luck charms—two Buddha statues and a picture of King Chulalongkorn—just like she did every night. The coffee finished brewing just as we finished cleanup, and I was pouring it into a thermos when my dad emerged from the kitchen, looking weary and grease-spattered, like he always does at the end of the night. He raised an eyebrow.

"We have coffee at home," he pointed out, rolling down the sleeves of his flannel shirt now that he was done cooking for the night.

"Eh, this is easier." I dumped a bunch of sugar into the thermos, followed by some half-and-half, then put the top on and mixed it around. My dad shook his head disapprovingly. "That much caffeine will stunt your growth."

"Dad," I said patiently, "I've been the same height since the seventh grade. I'm pretty sure the family genes stunted my growth a long time ago."

"No," Dad said. "Your brother is six feet tall." He smiled proudly at Nat, who stood on his tiptoes for a second and grinned back.

"Well, he stole all the good genes. Plus, I need this coffee for my history test tomorrow. Nat just saw me fall asleep standing up, didn't you, Nat?"

"I did," Nat said. "She looked like a freaking idiot."

My dad looked back and forth between the two of us

for a moment, trying to figure out if we were messing with him. Then he shrugged, reached into the mini fridge under the bar, and handed me two cans of Mountain Dew. "Okay. Study hard." He ruffled my hair and gently nudged me toward the front door as he turned off the dining room lights.

"Thanks, Dad." I smiled, putting my thermos of coffee under my arm. I popped open one of the cans right away and downed a huge swig. "I will."

And I would have, if I hadn't fallen asleep on my desk.

chapter two

The numbers on my blinking, beeping alarm clock were sideways from my perspective, since my head was resting on my desk in a puddle of drool. My eyes were open, but my brain wasn't quite functioning yet, so I stared glumly as the little red digits on the panda's stomach counted steadily forward. School started in forty-five . . . forty-four . . . forty-three minutes. At forty minutes, I attempted to move my head and succeeded only in moving my eyeballs, giving me a lovely view of the bed that hadn't been slept in and the piles of textbooks and papers from the night before strewn all over the carpet. Nat flung open the door and yelled, "*Alarm*, dumbass!" just as I was finally able to move my neck and stand up.

Everything was a blur after that, from finding questionably clean clothes on my floor, to cramming in a last-minute study session during homeroom, to completely missing the bell and having to race through the halls to make it to class on time.

"Oh my God, are you okay?" Sarah's round, porcelain-skinned face looked up at me as I sprinted through the door of our history classroom, where she was already set up with her usual test-taking paraphernalia: two hair clips doing their best to hold back her silky, long brown hair, two ballpoint pens, three #2 pencils, and a little carton of orange juice. "You look terrible," she said. Her arms were scrunched inside her sleeves as always, and her wide blue eyes got even wider when I threw my books on my desk, sat down, and then collapsed face-first onto them.

"Then I look how I feel," I mumbled into my notebook. "I fell asleep after work last night and didn't study for this like, at all."

Sarah patted my arm sympathetically. "Shut up," she teased. "I'm sure you'll do fine."

Yeah, well . . . I didn't.

"So much for Stanford," I said an hour later, after the carnage was over. "I'm gonna be slinging Tom Yum soup for the rest of my life." We gathered up our stuff and walked out of class, me looking shell-shocked, Sarah looking chipper.

"As previously mentioned, shut up," she said. "You always do this. You always panic prematurely."

"No, I don't," I said glumly, yanking out the pencil that I'd been using to hold my hair up and shaking the tangled bun loose.

"What'd you get on our freshman year Bio midterm?" Sarah asked.

"An A," I said.

"Sophomore year Government final?"

"A," I admitted, narrowing my eyes at her. I knew where this was going.

"Eighth grade first semester Social Studies presentation? Sixth grade science fair project? Third grade shoebox diorama on the rain forest? First grade book report on *Green Eggs and Ham*? Preschool finger-painting?"

"Yeah, yeah, all A's. You made your point," I said as she grinned at me cheerfully. "Doesn't mean I didn't still fail miserably just now. Good-bye, Stanford!" I said dramatically, pausing abruptly midstep to fling myself against a locker. Our school lockers are green, dingy, overwhelmingly covered in graffiti, and haven't been painted in about ten years, so I immediately regretted it and turned around so that I was facing the hallway.

"Shut up," Sarah said. "We're still getting into Stanford, we're still going, we're still rooming together, and that's the end of it. Fingers crossed," she added.

"*You're* going, Miss I-Could-Flunk-Everything-and-Still-Be-a-Shoo-In-for-Valedictorian. After that test, I won't be going anywhere but Miss Havisham's Hooker School for Delinquent . . . Hookers."

"You're not making any sense."

"That is very much the theme of this morning, yes."

Sarah took my arm and steered me toward the cafeteria, which was a pretty good idea, considering that the only thing I wanted to do was drown my sorrows in Cheetos. But we only managed to take two steps before we were waylaid by Leonard Chang, a sophomore who works for the school tutoring program with us. Harmless? Yes. Annoying? Totally.

"You're fired," Leonard said to me. He's exactly my height, and his face was very close to mine—I could see my reflection in the lenses of his round, black-framed glasses.

I backed away and stared at him, too zonked to figure out what the hell he could be talking about.

"Danny Gray just got an A on his last test and his parents don't want to pay for tutoring anymore, so he quit," Leonard explained in his slightly nasal, rapid-fire voice. "Which is just as well, because he was never gonna beat my G.P.A. anyway." He energetically pushed up the sleeves of the waffle weave he was wearing underneath his T-shirt before pulling them down again. "I just saw him in the tutoring office. He asked me to tell you. He didn't ask me to tell you that you look great today. But you look great today."

Sarah giggled and I tried not to roll my eyes. "Thanks,"

I said. Leonard tells me I look great about half the time he sees me. The other half of the time, he opts for "hot." It's sweet, but come on.

"By the way, did you hear that Mr. Dillman is hooking up with that new librarian-in-training?" he added. For a guy who has barely any friends, Leonard somehow knows everything that happens before anybody else.

"Ew, really?" Sarah said, and we exchanged a grossed-out glance.

"That's what I heard. I also heard that Taylor Spector got a nose job and is just pretending it was a basketball accident. Be sure to check him out when the bandages come off. Anyway, you should probably go over to the tutoring office and pick up a new student," Leonard said to me. "Not that you could ever beat my record of twelve students at once. I could walk you."

"That's cool, Leonard, but no thanks." I started inching away from him. Sarah, who'd already been inching, was already a few feet down the hall.

"Okay," said Leonard agreeably. "Hey, you know 'Maya, May I'?" I winced. I certainly did know it. It was a song he'd written (and, during a few awkward moments that I'd since been trying to forget, performed) for me last year. "I learned another chord, so it sounds a lot better now." He took off his glasses and breathed on them, then polished them with his shirt, squinted, and put them back on. "It's a four-chord song now. I'll play it for you sometime, if you remind me to bring my guitar—"

"Sure, that would be great. Later!" I said, running to catch up with Sarah, then grabbing her arm and walking as fast as I could away from Leonard. I made the mistake of glancing back and saw him energetically waving at me.

"He hearts you," Sarah said solemnly when we were out of earshot, then laughed.

"A year and counting," I said, shaking my head. Who knew that when I'd volunteered to train the new freshman tutor last year that he'd end up crushing on me this hard?

"Maybe he'll ask you to the Spring Fling," she continued, indicating the glittery poster we were passing in the hallway. It said, SWING THE FLING! and had a badly drawn picture of a Weston High Warrior dancing with a black silhouette of a woman in a flapper outfit.

"Great, I've always dreamed of bringing a date who looks like he's twelve," I said sarcastically.

"Oh, come on," Sarah giggled. "He looks thirteen, easy."

She was still giggling when we got to the tutoring office, but when I miserably plunked down onto the couch in the corner of the main room and went back to wearing my post-test shell-shocked face, she immediately shut up, sat down next to me, and passed me a conciliatory half-eaten bag of mini Oreos. She patted my arm as I snarfed them down.

"Come on," she murmured. "You didn't flunk."

"Maya, you look like medical waste," a voice piped up from behind her.

My friend Cat is not quite as nurturing.

I turned toward the row of study rooms lining the back wall of the tutoring office, from where Cat had just emerged. She gaped at me from behind her glasses of choice for the day, which were purple cat's-eye frames. She's got twenty-twenty vision, but she likes to make a statement. And today's, given the blue-streaked pigtails, the black and red fingernails, and the deliberately ripped black velvet skirt, was apparently "arty freak."

"Study amongst yourselves!" Cat snapped at the two confused-looking sophomores whom she'd left in the study room. She closed the door on them and threw herself onto the couch with me and Sarah. A little too enthusiastically— we were still disentangling ourselves when we heard the loud crash of a pile of books hitting the floor.

"That would be Jonny," said Cat. I looked up and saw our friend Jonathan just inside the doorway of the main room, picking up his books and a graphing calculator and frantically inspecting the latter for damage.

"Sorry," he said, pushing up his glasses and straightening out the front of his green button-down shirt. "In my defense, I wasn't being clumsy. It's just that I saw all you girls tangled up on the couch, and I got distracted." He grinned, absentmindedly patted his spiky blond hair, and disappeared into a study room to wait for Hilary, his favorite freshman. We were all convinced he was deliberately tutoring her badly in order to keep her in the program. The girl is fourteen and has a rack as big as my head. Or, I guess, two of my heads. If you want to get technical.

As Cat went back into her study room to finish tutoring her students, I got up off the couch and rang the bell at the window in the side wall where Mrs. Hunter, the school secretary who runs the tutoring program, usually sits. After a moment, Principal Davis appeared at it.

"Maya!" he roared. He looked like he wanted to jump through the window and give me a bear hug. Considering he is approximately the size of a Prius, I was glad he didn't.

"Oh," I said. "Hi, Principal Davis. Where's Mrs. Hunter?"

"On a break, on a break," he said jovially. "What can I do you for, smarty-pants?"

Smarty-pants? Seriously?

"I was wondering if you had anyone on the list," I said. "Leonard Chang just told me that Danny Gray quit because he got an A in Geometry."

"An A? Because of you? Wonderful! Of course, we'll get another student for you right away!" Principal Davis punched a few keys on Mrs. Hunter's computer. "How about Camden King?" he asked.

Ew. That guy.

"Is there anyone else?" I asked quickly. Principal Davis's hand was poised on the mouse, looking like it was ready to click a doom-sealing button.

"There is," he said, "but you're the only free tutor who's qualified to teach Algebra II."

"I just mean that Camden King is kind of—"

"Difficult? True. You'd be his sixth tutor in a month."

My eyes widened. "His *sixth* in a—"

"But if anyone can turn that boy around, it's you!" Principal Davis clicked the mouse, punched a few more keys on Mrs. Hunter's computer, and then grabbed a few sheets out of the printer. He stapled the papers to Camden's information folder and shoved it across the counter at me. "Remember, our cumulative G.P.A. is the third highest in the state. Our funding has almost doubled, thanks to students like you helping out students who are . . . not so much like you. So go forth and conquer, for the good of the school!"

He came out from behind the window, patted my shoulder energetically, and swept out the door past the returning Mrs. Hunter with a hearty "Tutor hard, everyone! Keep up the good work!"

Sarah and I rolled our eyes at each other as I sat back down on the couch next to her and stared at Camden's information folder with distaste. Technically I'd never spoken to him, but I'd seen him around school a lot, and I could believe the stories. His family is loaded, he's been popular since birth, and the license plate on his Escalade says PIMP CK. You know those guys who are really, really hot, but at the same time you're pretty sure they've got crabs? Colin Farrell comes to mind. And so does Camden King.

"Christ," I muttered, flipping through the folder and seeing various transcript pages with grades ranging from C– to F. "Are they serious?"

"Maybe they're confident you can handle him," Sarah said hopefully. She peered over my shoulder into the folder.

"That's not the point. The point is that I hate him . . . even though I've never met him." I looked up. "Is that wrong? Is that shallow?"

"No shallower than the shallow end of his giant back-yard swimming pool full of whores," Cat called through the cracked-open door of her study room.

"Thanks, I feel better," I said.

"No problem. It's what I do." She ducked her head back into the study room.

"Well," Sarah ventured, again trying to find the upside. "At least he's cute. I mean, he's tall . . . and he's got the body of a water polo player, and he doesn't even play water polo." She blushed a little as she said this, then deliberately let her long brown hair fall over her face.

"Irrelevant," I said glumly. "Being an ass trumps being

a piece of ass." I went back to looking through his information folder. "Wow, he's even dumber than I thought. No wonder all the other tutors quit on him."

"Come on, Maya." Sarah wasn't giving up. "We don't know who his other tutors were. Maybe he'll be really nice to you. Maybe it'll be . . . fun."

"*Suuure,*" I said.

"You know," Camden said as he walked up to the study room where I was waiting for him, "you should be wearing a tighter shirt."

He plunked down in the chair next to me, elbowed the door closed, and looked me over from head to toe.

"Uh . . . what?" I stared at him, hoping that either: a) I'd heard him wrong or b) I'd heard him right, but he had a reasonable explanation for his annoying comment, and that he was about to elaborate in a very polite manner.

He kicked his Pumas up onto the table and leaned back. "You're pretty cute, but you don't really have much going on up in this area," he said, waving his hands in the general direction of my chest. "Tighter would help. Emphasize what you *do* have." He put his feet back on the floor, glanced up and down at my outfit of jeans and a black crewneck sweater, and then turned to check out his own hazy reflection in the study room window. He yanked off his hoodie to expose a blue and gray ringer tee underneath, and then ran a hand through his purposeful bedhead of blondish-brown waves. I would've admired his biceps if he hadn't already been doing it himself.

"Maybe you should worry less about what I'm wearing and more about the fact that you're flunking Algebra," I said icily.

"I'm not flunking," Camden said, flinging his hoodie over the back of the chair next to him. "I'm getting a D. Didn't they give you all my info, uh . . ." He leaned over and looked at the cover of my notebook. "Mayo?"

"Maya."

"Whatever," he said. "Your handwriting sucks."

"As do your grades, so we should probably get started," I said, yanking my notebook away from him and taking out some pencils. "Do you have any homework you want to go through?"

"Homework? Sure," he said agreeably. I would have been surprised at the sudden attitude shift, except for the fact that it lasted about two seconds—his cell phone beeped, and he spent the next several minutes sending ten different texts to various people. Somewhere in the middle of the process, he pulled an algebra book out of his backpack with his non-texting hand and shoved it in my general direction without looking at me; it slid off the table and I leaned over to grab it.

"Nice butt," Camden said from behind me. I quickly sat up. "Too bad your personality doesn't match it," he added.

"And too bad your brains don't match your dad's bank account," I shot back. "If they did, we wouldn't be here."

Camden stared at me for a moment, opening his mouth and then closing it again before breaking into a grin. "Wow," he finally said as he got out a mechanical pencil and started clicking it noisily. "You're an interesting one. Most girls are so stunned by this whole business"—he waved the pencil at himself—"that they can't even attempt to be bitchy."

"Well, I'm not and I can," I said.

"I don't know if I like you or hate you."

"Hate me. It'll make us even," I said. "Now shut up and open your math book."

He raised an eyebrow, looking at me with what appeared to be half admiration and half desire to throw the book at my head, but by the time he started to say something, his phone beeped again with yet another text. He checked it, and then snapped his phone shut with finality.

"Sorry," he said, getting up and lazily stretching his arms over his head. "We're gonna have to reschedule this little shindig."

"Fine," I said, scooting back in my chair. "You still have to pay me for the hour."

"Not according to school policy, but nice try at swindling me." Camden grinned and threw down some cash anyway, then pocketed his cell phone and opened the study room door. "I'm off to sexually harass some cheerleaders." And with that, he peaced out.

I sat there for a minute, both angry and amused at what had just happened. Camden had not only lived up to his reputation, but he had actually surpassed it. I shuddered, pondering how horrific it would be the next time I had to hang out with him for more than ten minutes; eventually I decided to just be glad he was gone for the moment. Stuffing the relatively effortless fifteen bucks I'd just made into my pocket, I started to pack up my stuff, then saw that Camden had left his book bag. *Huh.* I casually bumped it with my hip on my way out, making it fall off the table.

Good thing the trash can was there to catch it.

chapter three

Thanks to Camden bailing early, I was able to finish all of my homework before my restaurant shift even started, and thanks to the speediness of machine test scanning, I found out I'd gotten an A– on my history test. Fine, so I'd been overly paranoid . . . but any senior year G.P.A. slippage could jeopardize the whole merit-based scholarship thing, so it wasn't like I could really slack off. At all.

And, as if I didn't have enough to worry about, my parents picked that night to spring the news that they were tacking a trade show onto their weekend trip to Washington, D.C. They'd been planning on driving down for a distant cousin's wedding for months, and it had been more or less agreed upon that I was going to be in charge while they were gone. But now that the trip was two days longer, they suddenly seemed wholly and completely convinced that I was going to screw something up.

"So why don't we just shut down while you're gone, and then you won't have to worry about it?" I asked as I sorted silverware behind the bar. A little vacation sounded pretty damn good to me.

"We cannot afford to give up five days of revenue," my mom snapped. "It is too bad, actually," she added in a gentler tone. "It would be nice for you to see a real Thai engagement party and wedding, but with school for you and Nat . . ."

"We could go if we flew," I suggested.

"We cannot afford that either," my mom sighed. She then launched into what was to become a full evening of making sure that my head contained all the necessary knowledge for keeping a restaurant afloat, including the avoidance of burning, flooding, explosion, implosion, and disintegration. I was setting up the table candles when she started with the trivia questions.

"What's item N4?" she asked, staring at me expectantly. I don't know why she bothered; I've had the entire menu memorized since I was six.

"Drunken Noodles," I answered.

She looked pleased that I'd answered so quickly. "Which of the soups can be made vegan?"

"Only the Gang Jeud Woon Sen," I said.

"What do you do if somebody complains that their meal is not good?"

"Apologize and offer them some free green-tea ice cream."

"Wrong!" she exclaimed. "You *smile* and apologize and offer them ice cream!"

"Okay, Mom."

"But only if they look like they might come back. If not, they can go to hell."

"*Okay*, Mom."

Satisfied for the time being, she went back to the kitchen to continue her last-minute supply check. I looked around. The dining room was still empty and it was already six-thirty. I crossed my fingers for an easy evening.

"Hey," Nat whispered, appearing at my shoulder from out of nowhere. "When Mom and Dad are gone, can I drive?"

My parents barely let *me* drive. When they took me to get my license on my sixteenth birthday, they promptly told me that I could only use the car in dire emergencies, like if both of them suddenly got all their limbs amputated. "Not blind, though. If we go blind, we still drive. You just direct us where to go."

"Yeah, you can drive," I told Nat.

His eyes lit up. "Sweet!" He gleefully punched the air in front of his face.

"Although I guess I should ride with you." He only had his learner's permit and was supposed to drive with a parent in the car for it not to be illegal, so we'd be breaking some laws anyway.

"Sucks!" he said.

I shrugged. "Better than nothing." He had to agree with that.

Finally, a few customers came in, and I took the pony-tail elastic off my wrist and put my hair up as my mom sat them in my section. A few other groups followed during the next hour or so, but they were small—twos and threes—and nicely spaced out, so we never got the usual mid-evening rush. It was my easiest night of work in months, actually . . . or it was until Camden King and three of his friends walked through the door.

I stopped dead—I'd been on the way over with a water pitcher—turned around, and kneeled behind the bar, peeking out just in time to see Camden and his pals plunk themselves down at a table in my section before my mom even got a chance to seat them there. After a minute, Nat wandered by, and I reached out and tugged on his pant leg. He looked down at me.

"Dude, what the—?"

"Shhh," I hissed.

"What are you doing on the floor?"

"See those guys over there? They're from school."

I watched as Nat took a look around the dining room. "Who?"

"They're my year," I said. "It's Camden King and some other guys."

Nat heard the name and spotted them at the exact same moment, and he recoiled. "Lemme guess. You want me to switch with you? No freakin' way."

"Please?" I begged. "It's less embarrassing for you. You've never talked to him before."

"What, like you have?" Nat asked.

"Yeah, I was tutoring him in Algebra earlier today, so—"

"So you know him. Good for you. Go deal. Besides, didn't you used to like that one guy?"

I peeked out over the bar and saw Camden's friend Derek Rowe, who was admittedly kind of rocking his slightly-too-small vintage tee. "That was the fifth grade!" I said defensively. "Plus, I stopped as soon as I found out he was beating you up every day for no rea—Oooh, that's why you don't want to switch with me."

"Exactly." Nat yanked me up from the floor and shoved me out in front of the bar, and I slowly started making my way toward the Table of Doom. Besides Camden and Derek, there were two lacrosse guys, Brad Slater and Dave Markley, which meant that the combined I.Q. of the table was probably . . . four.

"Hello!" I said as cheerfully as I could muster. Out of the corner of my eye, I could see my mom watching me.

"Oh," Camden said, surprised. "It's you." He tilted his

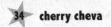

chair back for a moment to look at me, then let it settle back onto the floor.

"Yeah, it's me," I said. I wanted to add, "And now I will be kicking your sorry butts out," but that would've been shoddy waitressing.

"Dude, you know her?" Brad asked. He inspected me from under his hoodie, then slid the hood off of his head and inspected me from out in the open.

"I guess, as of this afternoon," Camden said, reaching lazily across the table toward the little metal stand that contained a Singha ad on one side and our recent menu additions on the other. He looked at the Singha side and suddenly perked up. "Hey, can you serve us beer?"

The other guys snickered. I smiled politely. "No."

"Even if we have ID?" Dave asked with a smirk. He reached into his pocket and started pulling out his wallet.

"Well, here's the thing," I said. I could see my mom frowning as she arranged a pile of menus on the counter into a neat stack, and I knew I had about five seconds before she started barking at me not to leave my other tables hanging. "If you show me your fake IDs, I'm supposed to confiscate them. So you're probably better off just ordering a Coke or something."

"Aw, come on," wheedled Camden. "Can't you do us a favor?"

"Camden," I said flatly, "why on earth would you think that I'd *ever* want to do *you* a favor?"

A chorus of "ooohs" and muffled snickers emanated from his friends. "Wow," Dave said. "She's like, sassy."

"For now," Camden said, and looked up at me. "But you're here to service us, aren't you?" He high-fived Brad, and I forced a smile.

"Yes, that's what I'm here for. Service." I struggled to keep smiling, knowing my mom was watching me intently. "How about I give you a few minutes to decide what you want, and I'll come back?"

I practically sprinted away from them as my mom accosted me at the end of the bar. "Why are you chitchatting with boys when there are other customers who need your help?" she asked. Her tone of voice was so innocent that it basically veered right back around into sounding suspicious.

"Sorry, Mom," I said. "Those guys go to my school, and I was just—"

"Don't forget there are other tables."

"I know, Mom. I'm sorry."

She sighed. "Okay. But remember, you cannot let this place get out of control, especially when we are gone." She shot me a half-warning, half-sympathetic glance, and then turned on a dime to smile brilliantly at a customer who had come in to pick up his takeout order. I went behind the bar, where Nat was putting a sprig of mint into a glass of lime soda, and smacked him on the head with a menu.

"That's professional," he said dryly. He grabbed the menu out of my hand.

"Shut up," I said. "The next hour—or however long it takes those guys to eat—is gonna be hell for me, and if you think I'm not going to take it out on my little brother, you're stupider than *they* look."

I braced myself for the nightmare of taking the guys' orders and returned to their table, where I was greeted by the sight of Derek and Brad shooting spitballs at each other. I cleared my throat. "Ready to order?"

"Absolutely, serving wench," Dave said. He was still wearing his letter jacket, even though his face was slightly pink, and he kept tugging at the collar of the sweatshirt he was wearing underneath.

"Oh, dude," Derek said. "Serving wench! That's hilarious, man." He was talking really loudly, and our other customers were beginning to glance over at their table. If this kept up, it was going to progress to extended hostile stares, and then to complaining to management. My mom seemed to sense this and waved me over.

"Yeah?" I asked her. "I was just about to take their order."

"Your friends are disturbing other customers," she pointed out flatly.

"They're not my friends, and I know," I said. "I'm try-ing to make them stop."

"Try harder."

Sigh. I went back over, bracing myself for another round of "Hey, serving wench!" or worse.

"So," Camden asked conversationally, "do you ever get naked and let people eat sushi off of your body?"

"Sushi, Japanese. This restaurant, Thai," I said, taking out a pen. "Are you and the Three Muske*queers* ready to order?"

Camden raised an eyebrow and choked back a laugh as the other guys glared, but they managed to fire off a list of seven dishes and three appetizers, in between discreet swigs of the flask they kept "hidden" under the table.

"Thanks," I said, putting my pen back in my pocket. "I'll get that started for you, and is there anything else I can get you?"

Dave purposefully knocked over his water glass. "Yeah. Can I get some more water?"

I watched as the water cascaded across the table, drenched a menu, then spilled onto the floor, soaking rap-idly into the carpet. Derek and Brad, who were in the water's path, scooched their chairs back so quickly that they jostled the people at the next table.

"Sorry," they both said, laughing. The people gave

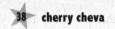

them dirty looks, and then turned the looks toward me, too. Way to shoot the non-messenger.

"Let me get something to clean that up, and I'll be right back with more water," I said through gritted teeth. I grabbed a few napkins off an empty table and threw them over the puddle to try and stem the tide. As I walked away, I could still hear them yelling.

"Thanks, serving wench!" Dave said in a singsong voice.

"You should smile more, wench!" Brad echoed.

"Yeah, or else we might have to stiff you on the tip!" Derek called.

"Dude, did you just say *stiff*?" Dave asked.

"Or we might have to drop a negative comment in your suggestion box!" Derek added.

"Did you just say suggestion box?"

"I bet her box loves suggestions," Brad snickered. More high fives all around. For Chrissakes. I cleaned up the spill, refilled everyone's water, and assured my mom, who was now looking genuinely worried instead of just irritated, that I had the situation under control.

Until Derek grabbed a menu, ripped out a page, rolled it up, and put the end into one of the table candles to make a torch.

Oh, *hell* no.

I ran over and reached out to grab the now-flaming

page, but Camden's hand got there first. He yanked the burning paper out of the candle and dunked it in Derek's water glass.

"Hey, what the—I was drinking that!" Derek shoved Camden's shoulder.

"You still can," Camden pointed out calmly. He jerked his head toward the cash register, indicating my mom, who had her hand threateningly poised over the phone. "Quit being a jerk."

Derek paused, visibly straining to think of something clever to say. He eventually came out with the always reliable "Screw you, man!"

Camden ignored him and handed me the mutilated menu. "Sorry about that," he said, looking up at me. He must've seen the stricken look on my face because he added, "Uh, can I pay for it or something?"

"It's pretty much just made of paper," I said, inhaling deeply to try and calm down. I started walking toward the bar so I could throw the menu in the trash.

"You sure?" Camden called. He got up and followed me.

"It's fine, whatever. Forget it," I said, my panic dissipating now that the restaurant no longer appeared to be in danger of burning down. "We have extras." I chucked the sodden, blackened mass of former menu in the garbage. "If you really want to do me a favor, go sit down and get your stupid friends to chill."

Camden studied me for a second. "Okay," he said. And the next time I looked over, they'd stopped.

Huh.

"I might be crazy," I said to Nat as I went back to the kitchen to put in their orders, "but I think Camden was being marginally less of a jerk than his friends were just now."

"Really?" Nat said. "Didn't know that was possible."

"Yeah. And I was gonna spit in his food, but now I'm thinking I shouldn't." I paused to ponder it—it's not something I've ever actually done—as I stuck their order slip into the metal rack above the prep table. "Eh, I can still spit in Derek's."

Nat grinned and theatrically cleared his throat. "Holler when it's ready, because I want to help."

chapter four

And that was the last I ever saw of Camden King.

Well, until the next day, when he hunted me down at my locker after school. The hallway was crowded with people rushing to catch the bus, and I got jostled several times as I finished packing my grungy backpack that I've had since like, fourth grade. I slammed my locker door and practically had a heart attack when I saw Camden on the other side of it.

"Hi," he said. He was wearing a brightly striped polo shirt under a gray fleece, and was standing so close to me that all I could see was alternating orange and blue.

"'Bye," I answered, as I scooched away and attempted to walk past him. He blocked my dramatic exit by stepping into my path, causing me to sort of run into him and bounce off his chest. Graceful.

"Sorry again about last night," he said. He put his

hands in his pockets and looked down at me, stepping a little bit closer as someone came barreling down the hallway with a library cart full of books.

"Hey, I was just surprised that your friends were able to outdo you," I said.

"Yeah, well, I just didn't want you to spit in my food."

I tried to keep a straight face and failed miserably. He stared at me for a second, then realized. "Oh, dude, you didn't."

"You'll never know for sure," I said, and smiled.

He glared at me. "I'm gonna tell everyone I know that your restaurant sucks and that they shouldn't go there."

"Oh, come on," I said, trying to sound like I didn't care. I looked around quickly to see if anyone passing by had heard him, but aside from a random glance or two, nobody seemed to be paying much attention.

"You're lucky we aren't all going to sue," he added.

"*You're* lucky I didn't call the cops when your friend tried to burn down the building," I snapped.

"He was just having fun," Camden said. "Maybe you've heard of it?"

"Heard of it. Enjoy it. At the moment, not having it." I turned to go. Camden took a step around me and managed to block my exit again.

"Hey, so were you gonna help me with my Algebra or what?" he asked, leaning sideways onto a locker door.

"I tried to do that yesterday," I pointed out. "You took off."

"Something came up," he said. "I'm free right now, though. Want to do it now?"

"No," I said. "Or ever," I added for good measure.

"What, you're quitting on me already? You can't do that. Come on." He grabbed the strap of my backpack and started pulling me down the hallway as I struggled to disengage myself. Several kids stared at us, including Dani Davis and Stacey Ray. You'd think since Dani's dad is the principal, she would be *more* paranoid about showing that much torso on a school day, but it actually had the opposite effect; she was wearing extremely low-rise jeans and a sweater that ended three inches above her navel. As for Stacey, who was wearing a miniskirt and sandals even though it was forty degrees outside, I don't know what her excuse was. "Hey, C. K.," they giggled in unison as we passed by them.

"Ladies," Camden said, flashing them a smile. He glanced approvingly at both their belly rings, but he didn't slow down.

I attempted to ground my feet on the floor to stop him. It didn't work—not surprising, since he's over a foot taller than me and God knows how much heavier—so I grabbed his fingers and started trying to pry them off of my backpack strap.

"What the hell are you doing?" I demanded.

He kept yanking me along, his long strides moving us quickly down the hallway. "If you quit now, we'll both just have to go back to that stupid office and get stuck with someone even lamer—"

"Not sure if that's possible," I said.

"Anything's possible," he answered.

"No, seriously. I'm pretty sure anybody would be better than you."

"Yeah, hilarious. I'll pay double for this afternoon. How's that?"

Ah, the language of money. "Fine," I said, shrugging myself out of my backpack and beginning to follow him of my own accord. He was walking even faster now, and we were almost to the stairs that led down to one of the school's back doors; I had to trot to keep up. "Let's go to the tutoring office. I've got a few hours before I have to be at work, and—"

"The tutoring office is for pussies," Camden said.

"The library?" I suggested. "We could use a study room." Camden sped up yet again, so I had to as well. He was still holding on to my backpack strap.

"We'll figure it out in the car," he said, pushing me through the door to the student parking lot. I grimaced as the cold outside air hit me, and I wrapped my coat tighter around myself. "Besides," he added, "you owe me for chucking my book bag into the trash yesterday."

"I didn't do that. . . . Okay, I totally did that," I said.

"Exactly," he answered. "So suck it up. We're going where I want." Which is how, two minutes later, I found myself standing next to Camden's ridiculously over-pimped gas-guzzler of a black Escalade, then sitting in it after he threw open the door and prodded me into the passenger seat. The interior was black leather, with a custom G.P.S. screen built into the dash, a flip-down DVD screen in the ceiling, and multiple random gadgets I couldn't identify. Through the cracked-open window, I heard some guy walking by mutter to his friend, "Wow, is Cam King slumming with the nerd chicks now, or what?" I made a move for the door, and the locks clicked. Camden grinned at me.

"Where are we going?" I asked, giving up and fastening my seat belt. If I was going to get in trouble for being in a guy's car, I figured I shouldn't add injury to injury by smashing my face through the windshield.

"I dunno. My house, I guess," he answered. He was fiddling intently with his iTrip, banging it several times against the dashboard before it finally started working. The stereo suddenly blasted Kanye so loudly, I could barely hear myself talk.

"My parents are going to kill me," I shouted.

"What?" he yelled back, turning down the music.

"I said, my parents are going to kill me." I reached up and pulled my hair out from where it had gotten pinned between my back and the seat.

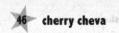

"Huh? Why?" Camden asked. He looked genuinely puzzled.

"Well, aside from the fact that I'm supposed to either go straight home or straight to the restaurant after school unless I'm tutoring, they're totally paranoid about me going to random people's houses." Outside the window, I saw Brad Slater walk by on his way toward his car. He did a double take when he saw that I was sitting in Camden's passenger seat.

"Dude, that's really freakin' weird," Camden said.

"You're telling me." Wait, I had just agreed with him. Ew. "But anyway," I added quickly, "I'll get in trouble if we go to your house. Can we just like, go to Starbucks or something?"

"You have a cell phone, don't you?" he asked. I nodded and pulled it out of my backpack. "Well, the whole point of a cell phone is that when people call you, you can lie about where you are."

"I don't know. My parents are pretty good at figuring out—"

"Oh my God!" he exclaimed, rolling his eyes. "You've never even tried it, have you?" He looked at me, mouth slightly open in disbelief.

I suddenly felt very lame. Then I felt lame for feeling lame. Then my phone rang.

"It's my mom," I squeaked, not picking it up. A few

months ago, Nat had changed the ring for her on both our phones to "Mama Said Knock You Out." At the time, it had cracked us both up, but now it was striking fear into my heart.

"Good, now's your chance." Camden turned the key in the ignition, backed up out of the parking space, and gunned the car out of the parking lot. I glared at him as I flipped open my phone.

"Hel—hello?" I couldn't hide my nervousness.

"What is all that noise?" my mom asked.

I frantically motioned for Camden to turn down his music even further. "Uh, nothing. Somebody just walked by with a really noisy iPod." Camden turned the volume down, then turned it way up for a split second, then back down, this time all the way. I slapped his hand and glared at him. He grinned as he pulled out of our school's back driveway and onto the street.

"Where are you?" my mom asked.

"The library?" I winced, looking out the window of Camden's car at what was very much the football field behind the school and not the library.

"Okay . . . well, I want to go over the schedule with you again for when we are gone, so . . . see you at four-thirty." She sounded extremely suspicious, but at least she had hung up. I breathed a sigh of relief and turned to see Camden laughing at me.

"You are the world's *worst* liar," he said. He turned the music back on and absentmindedly drummed his fingers on the steering wheel.

"Thank you. I love being driven somewhere against my will and then insulted," I said, looking out the window. The football field and track, then houses, then trees, then the bridge over the river and the golf course, all positively whizzed by—Camden was driving sixty in a forty zone. "Uh . . . do you have a radar detector in this thing?"

"Of course," he said, speeding up to eighty for no reason before screeching to a halt at a red light, then slamming his foot on the accelerator again the second it turned green.

The area immediately surrounding Weston High is filled with smaller houses like mine, but Camden had been speeding so much that we were already miles away. Here the houses were bigger, the lawns more extensive, the garages three-car instead of two-car. He started to turn into a really fancy gated neighborhood called Arbor Pointe, according to the big granite boulder by the security booth, but then he stopped and kept the car going straight instead.

I looked at him. "What, did you forget where you live?"

"We need to make a few pit stops first."

He started heading toward downtown, driving sixty all the way to EZ Wash, where we churned through a complete wash and wax. "Your car was like, perfectly clean already," I pointed out.

"And now it's perfecter and cleaner," he answered, driving seventy all the way to McDonald's, where he ordered himself a Value Meal, then told the woman working the window that she had "the most beautiful eyes I've ever seen" in order to score extra fries.

"That chick was like, fifty," I said.

"And that's why the line worked on her," he answered.

After that we went to the drive-through liquor store, where he bought a bottle of Maker's Mark with a fake ID—although it didn't seem necessary, considering that the tattooed guy with the shaved head at the window greeted him with a friendly "What up, C?" and the amount of cash Camden gave him was well over what the bottle actually cost. Finally, he turned the car around and appeared to be heading back to his house, albeit the long way; we were practically at the mall on the opposite side of town by now, and he looked like he was about to purposely wind around the streets of downtown instead of taking Main Street right through. I glanced at my watch. Great—I had to be at work in an hour. Maybe it was actually good that he was speeding like a maniac.

"Oh, dude, dude, dude . . ." Camden suddenly started braking.

"What now?" I asked, annoyed.

Camden slowed the car to a crawl and stared out the window. "Track chicks," he said reverently.

I followed his gaze. Indeed, we were just outside the field of Pembroke, our rival high school, where the girls' track team was lining up to start what looked like a sprint drill. They were wearing those very short track team shorts, although a few of them were still acknowledging the early spring cold by wearing spandex leggings underneath. The ones that weren't lined up yet were jogging in place or stretching, and Camden was staring appreciatively.

"That's it, I'm getting out of the car," I said. I unbuckled my seat belt.

"Oh sure, you really have the balls to jump out of a moving vehicle," he said, not taking his eyes off of the track girls.

"It's not moving right now," I pointed out, and reached for the door handle. He immediately stepped on the gas and moved the car two feet forward, then slammed on the brakes. My backpack and books slid off my lap and landed at my feet.

"Ow!" I take a lot of A.P. classes and let me tell you, the textbooks aren't exactly the world's lightest. "What the hell are you doing?"

"Just showing you that there's no way you're gonna pull off some sort of Lara Croft escape maneuver."

I reached for the door handle again, but he immediately

repeated his trick, causing me to slide forward and hit the dashboard.

"Ow! I could call the cops," I said, rubbing my elbow. "This is kidnapping or something."

"Please, like anyone would believe that," he said, grinning. "Want me to kiss your wound and make it better?" He reached for my elbow and I shrank away.

"I have to be at work soon," I snapped.

"Noted." He stepped on the gas again as I struggled to put my seat belt back on, and before I knew it, we were pulling into the big circular driveway in front of his house. Or mansion, more like—my own house could probably have fit in his front hall, which showcased a huge, curving staircase, a marble floor, and a giant, intricate, very glittery chandelier. It was extremely warm inside; his family clearly had no problem jacking up the heat, whereas my parents always insist on setting the thermostat so low that I wear my coat inside the house half the time. I followed Camden to his kitchen, the entirety of which was a shiny, gleaming black, just like his car. He opened some cupboards and fished out bags of SunChips, Doritos, Oreos, and Pop-Tarts, all of which he held out to me. I shook my head.

"Okay." He shrugged. "Let's go down to the basement." He pulled off his fleece and started out of the kitchen.

I didn't move. "How do I know you're not some

kind of serial killer with a perverted sex dungeon down there?"

He grinned at me. "Well . . . I'm not a serial killer."

"So says you." I trudged down the carpeted staircase after him. "But Ted Bundy was apparently very popular in his day, and just so you know, I've got my keys in between my fingers right now, which means that if you try anything, I can totally punch you and stab you at the same time, and—oh my God, it's like freakin' Narnia down here!"

We were at the bottom of the stairs, and Camden had flung open the door to his basement. I glanced around and saw a glass-enclosed workout room with a bike, an elliptical, a rowing machine, and about a zillion free weights; a pool table with a giant KING PROPERTIES, INC. logo in the middle; a door that was slightly ajar and through which I could see a few rows of home theater seats and a giant screen; a wet bar; a hot tub; and a guy taking his clothes off and getting into said hot tub.

Wait a minute.

"Uh, Camden?"

"Yeah?" he asked.

"What are you *doing*?"

"What?" he said. "I can't study if I'm not relaxed. This relaxes me."

Down to a pair of blue boxers, Camden got into the

water. I noted the six-pack and then mentally kicked myself for noting the six-pack. Then I noted the pecs and mentally kicked myself again. The arms, I'd noted before. I mentally punched myself in the head for that one.

"Hop in," he said, eyes closed as he slid in up to his neck, resting the back of his head against the edge of the hot tub.

"Yeah . . . no," I answered. I took off my backpack and coat and let them drop to the floor, but I didn't move any closer.

"Come on," he said, still with his eyes closed. "There's probably a bikini lying around here somewhere from last weekend. I threw this awesome party, you should have— nah, you shouldn't have came."

"Wouldn't have wanted to," I agreed.

Camden opened his eyes and studied me. "Seriously, though, get in. We can just put our books on the edge here." He reached into a mini fridge that was next to the hot tub and cracked open a Red Bull, then indicated the seating area around the hot tub.

"No!" I exclaimed, remaining standing. I pondered just leaving. Of course, I couldn't really figure out how I was going to get back to school in time for my mom to pick me up without Camden driving me, so I was actually kind of stuck.

"Okay, stay in there if you want to. But I'm staying out

here." I walked over, reached into his book bag, took out his Algebra book, and then sat down. "We'll make this fast. How long does it usually take you to do your problem sets?"

"No idea. I don't usually do them. How long does it take you?"

I looked at his assignment sheet. It was ridiculously easy. "Like, ten minutes," I said.

"Cool. Then how about you do this assignment for me, and I'll pay you a hundred bucks?"

"What? No!"

Was he crazy?

"Why not?" he asked.

"Because that's cheating!" I exclaimed.

"Come on. What do you usually make at tutoring, fifteen bucks an hour? And you could make a hundred in ten minutes. I thought you people were supposed to be good at math."

"Yes, my *people* all do math for fun, while simultaneously dry-cleaning our karate outfits and giving each other manicures and pedicures, all in between our numerous piano and violin recitals," I said, slamming his book shut. "Do your own freaking work. Although I guess that's a completely foreign concept to you, isn't it? Since you've been deep-throating a silver spoon your whole life."

"That is so hot that you just said that," Camden said,

lazily swigging his Red Bull. "Besides, I'll work one of these days when I have to. I'll either go into real estate like my dad or find some rich old widow who wants . . . uh . . . services."

"That doesn't sound like work," I said.

"Of course it is, if she's *old*," he answered.

I had to smile at that one, and he took the opportunity to forge ahead. "So, will you do this problem set for me? It'll save us both time. And you know, my friends would probably want in, so you could potentially make a ton of—"

"For the last time, no!" I crossed my arms and glared at him.

Camden sighed. "Fine. Read the first question out loud, will you?"

Finally. I turned to the correct page and was starting to read when my phone rang.

It was my mom. *Eeep.*

"Hi, Mom," I half-whispered, trying to sound calm and bored, as if I were in the library.

"You are not in the library," she said. I felt all the blood drain from my face. "I called the school library and the librarian says you are not there right now," she continued.

"What? I am too," I said defensively. I could see Camden listening in on my half of the conversation and beginning to smirk. "She just . . . she doesn't know what I look like."

"She says there are no Asians in the library right now."

"There are always Asians in a school library; that's where most of us live," I exclaimed. Silence from my mom; a snicker from Camden. "I was probably in the bathroom when she was looking," I said quickly, trying to cover. "I'm here. She just didn't see me."

"Okay. I am coming to get you," Mom said, and hung up.

I shut my phone and looked at Camden in a panic. "Oh my God, you have to get me out of—"

"Your clothes?" he interrupted. "Sure. You've probably got a sexy little bra happening under there." He reached for the edge of my shirt, and I jumped up and reached for my backpack.

"Yeah, yeah, very funny, but no. I mean out of *here*! My mom is coming to pick me up *right now*, and I'm supposed to be at the library! You have to drive me back to school!" I flung my arms into my coat and then through my backpack straps.

"Dude, just calm down and call her back. Put me on the phone. I'll pretend I'm a student teacher—"

"No! We have to go *now*! *Please!*" I stared at him, my eyes simultaneously angry and begging.

"Okay," he said, as he got out of the hot tub.

Naked.

I squeaked in horror and turned away; the boxers from before had apparently made a run for the border. Camden laughed and put on a towel.

"Told you I like to be comfortable when I study." He grabbed his car keys and his clothes. "Let's go."

We sped like hell all the way to school, Camden every once in a while glancing over at my panicked face and white knuckles clutching my backpack and telling me to chill out. I ignored him and prayed the entire time that my mom would drive over a nail and get a flat tire, or that there would be a massive multi-car fender bender in her path (no injuries, of course), or that she would forget something and have to drive back and get it. The Escalade screeched past a kid on a bike and into the driveway in front of the WESTON HIGH sign, and I was overjoyed to see that my mother's car wasn't there yet—we'd gotten back in time. I unbuckled my seat belt with one hand and opened the car door with the other.

"What, no thank you?" Camden asked.

I gaped at him as I hung halfway off of my seat. "For *what*?!"

"For the superior driving skills that got you back in time."

"Are you *serious*?" I said sarcastically. "Okay, fine. Thanks for saving my life, although first you almost ruined it."

"Welcome," Camden said cheerfully, ignoring the second half of what I'd said. "Maybe next time we'll actually get some work done." He grinned, ran his hand through his wet hair, and then playfully flicked the water at me.

"Maybe." I got out of his car. "But probably not, because I quit."

I glared at him, slammed the door, walked away, and didn't look back.

chapter five

"You are in charge all weekend," Dad said as we stood in the empty restaurant on Saturday morning, after going over a bunch of last-minute management details: time cards, cash register accounting, ingredient substitutions in case we ran out of something, the phone and fax numbers for our contacts at Sysco Food Delivery. "Monday through Wednesday, Krai and the rest of the staff will take care of lunch, but you come here right after school for dinner." He looked around for my brother. "Nat!"

"Yeah?" Nat asked, appearing from the kitchen. He was gnawing on half a mango, seemingly unperturbed by the juice dripping onto his watch.

"Watch," I said.

"Waterproof," he answered.

"Nat, listen to your sister while we are gone," my dad said. "She is Mom and Dad for the next few days." He handed me the keys to the restaurant and an envelope that was almost completely covered by a note that said "Emergency Money! Do not spend under any circumstance (unless emergency)" in Magic Marker. Awesome.

I grinned at Nat, who rolled his eyes a little at the prospect of someone only a year older than him being in charge, but he couldn't help grinning as well. This was the first time they'd ever left us home alone, and while we were obviously going to have to work our normal hours at the restaurant, the thought of having no curfew—and that I'd be able to leave work and go out with my friends for as long as I wanted instead of only an hour or so—gave me a fizzy feeling of happiness and a sudden desire to bounce on my tiptoes every few minutes.

I'd had to deal with some annoying fallout from my dramatic slamming of Camden King's car door two days ago—namely, he'd somehow managed to get my cell phone number and was sending me multiple texts, ranging from *hey, u didnt really quit on me did u?* to *give me a call this weekend* to *ok whatever I did, sorry I guess* to *dont b like this, mayo*—none of which I bothered answering. But that thorn in my side was shrinking by the minute, compared to the five days of absolute freedom coming my way. Well, freedom and *major* responsibility, but I was trying to look on the bright side.

"Be good," my mom said, giving me a hug and actually

looking a little teary. She blinked rapidly and shook her head as if she realized she was being silly.

"We will!" I said, hugging her back. Nat helped my dad load the little blue Prizm with a few bags of food in take-out containers, a black duffel bag, and the battered suitcases that they'd brought over when they first moved from Thailand. Then he and I watched, shivering in the slight flurries of early March snow that were coming down, as they got in and drove off, Mom waving enthusiastically through the back window until they were several blocks away and had disappeared out of sight.

Yes! They were gone! We were free! We could do anything we wanted! We could—

My cell phone started playing a tinny version of "Papa Don't Preach." Nat had apparently been on another ringtone spree. I flipped it open as he and I hurried back inside the restaurant, where it was warmer.

"Hi, Dad," I said. Nat raised his eyebrows and I gave him a "Duh, of course they're calling already" shrug.

"Just seeing if everything is okay," he said. I could hear my mom in the background telling him to tell me to tell Nat to double-check the back door lock.

"Everything is fine, Dad," I said. "You left thirty seconds ago."

"Yes, but your mom wanted to call. Okay. Good luck."

"Thanks. Drive safe," I said, thinking of the snow

flurries . . . although, looking out the window, I realized that they had already petered out almost completely.

"Thank you. 'Bye." My dad hung up. *Hmmm*. If they were going to call every five minutes, the next few days were going to be a lot less fun.

Nat and I set up the restaurant that morning with military precision; we straightened tablecloths, polished silverware, and refilled the water in the tiny bud vases on every table as if our parents were still there, yelling orders at us. Then, shortly before the lunch shift started, I opened the giant walk-in freezer in the kitchen to find Nat making out with a girl. A hot girl. A girl who looked like a shorter version of Tyra Banks, actually, except this girl was wearing trendy-yet-nerdy black-framed glasses and a distinctly *not* sexy Catholic school uniform under her gray peacoat.

"*Ahem*," I said. They jumped apart. Nat looked embarrassed. Short Nerdy Tyra did not.

"Oh, hey," said Nat. "Uh, Star, this is my sister, Maya. Maya, Star."

"Hi," I said. I shook the hand that Star held out to me, and then watched as she returned it to where it had been, which was my brother's back pocket. Christ. How did my little brother find the time to date when I couldn't? Wait a minute. How did my little brother find the *people* to date when I couldn't? Fighting the urge to simultaneously vomit and laugh, I asked Nat, "Can I talk to you outside for a second?"

"Sure," he said. He came out of the freezer, and Star followed him, pushing the door closed with her foot when it got stuck. She started to gamely make small talk with Krai, who just looked annoyed at her attempt. I yanked Nat through the swinging kitchen doors and out to the front of the restaurant.

"Dude, what the hell?" I asked. "Since when are you dating her? Since when are you *dating*?"

He shrugged. "We've been together for a few months. I figured there was no point in sneaking around when Mom and Dad aren't here."

"Where does she go to school?"

"Detroit Mercy. We met at Regionals."

"Wow," I said. "Leave it to you to pick up a girl at a Science Olympiad competition."

"I'm the studliest of nerds," he deadpanned, pushing up his glasses. "Wait a minute," he added suddenly. "You're not gonna tell on me, are you?"

"Of course not!" I laughed. "Unless I feel like it," I added ominously.

"That's not funny," Nat said.

"Not to you." He really didn't need to worry—the last time I ratted him out to our parents had been years ago, and only then because it had involved him microwaving my *Justified* CD—but it was fun to make him think he did. Especially since I was the one responsible for getting us through five days of restaurant operation alive.

The Saturday lunch shift went pretty decently. It was really, really crowded, and while it didn't exactly help that my parents called four times to demand a status report (especially when I was already on another call taking an order and had to flip back and forth between lines), things more or less went off without a hitch.

Dinner that night was cool as well; I accidentally gave somebody ten bucks too much change when they came to pick up their takeout, but they were nice enough to point it out. Plus, it was kind of dead for a Saturday night, so I got out in plenty of time for me, Sarah, Cat, and Jonny to go to the movies, disagree completely about which one to see, attempt to rent one, disagree again, and then end up just hanging out in the parking lot of the twenty-four-hour Meijers until two in the morning.

By Sunday lunch, I was pleasantly sleepy, having stayed out as late as I wanted to the previous night. We ran out of both cilantro and basil, so Nat had to run to the store for more while I held down the fort. The illegality of him driving by himself was outweighed by his fantastic mood at getting to drive by himself, and he came back without any problems, so that turned out fine.

Sunday dinner, on the other hand . . . not so much.

The very first people who walked in, a crabby-looking middle-aged couple, asked me to lower the music volume. An easy enough request, until half an hour later, when a group of already-tipsy college kids asked me to turn it up. I tried to split the difference but only managed to get dirty looks from both tables instead. This distracted me enough that I accidentally switched some customers' bags when they came in to pick up their takeout, and I had to field two different complaint calls fifteen minutes later. Neither party was motivated enough to drive back and get their free replacement food, thank God.

Then, some crazy wine connoisseur accused me of opening his bottle of Chardonnay incorrectly, and there was a momentary panic when the sliding metal door to the dishwasher jammed. Krai managed to pry it open with a fork—thereby breaking the fork, but we all figured a broken fork is better than a useless dishwasher.

So by the tail end of the evening, I was already pretty frazzled when Nat came over to the cash register and muttered unhappily, "Uh, that lady over there just asked to talk to the manager"—he pointed toward a pinched-looking woman in the back corner—"and the manager would be you."

"What's her problem?" I asked.

"What isn't?" He shrugged and practically sprinted back to the kitchen, which didn't bode well.

I sighed, smoothed out my apron and fixed my ponytail, and then went over to the table of two middle-aged women, both of whom looked pretty angry.

"Hi," I said, looking back and forth between them. "Can I help you with something?"

"Yes," said Angry Lady #1, glaring at me through her bifocals. "Our orders are wrong. We both ordered the Vegetarian Red Curry, and I don't think this is vegetarian." She pointed accusingly at her curry bowl with a long red fingernail.

"Oh, I'm sorry about that," I said, giving them an apologetic smile. "I'll have the kitchen fix that right up for you."

The curry looked pretty damn vegetarian to me—nothing but green peppers, eggplant, and tofu—and Krai gave me the world's most withering look when I checked with him. "They ask for it veggie. I made it veggie," he complained.

Nonetheless, my parents are all about placating the customer, so the easiest thing to do was have him whip up another batch; it didn't take long, and the women appeared mollified when I set the fragrant, steaming new bowls down in front of them. They started digging into it right away, both shaking their heads irritably when I asked them if they needed anything else.

Of course, twenty minutes later, when the two women

were the only people left in the restaurant, and Nat and I were both positively itching to turn the lights up and bust out the vacuum cleaner, they flagged me down again.

"Sooo sorry to bother you, sweetie, but this is the second time in a row you got our order wrong," said Angry Lady #1's passive-aggressive friend. "We asked for this curry to be vegan." She put her spoon down, leaned back in her chair, and stared up at me expectantly.

"Oh, I'm sorry," I said, struggling for politeness and picturing my mother yelling at me to make the customers happy. "I think you said vegetarian last time, actually, but this curry is vegan as well. It's made with coconut milk."

"Was it made in a separate pot?"

"Yes," I said. "I think so." Out of the corner of my eye, I could see Nat approaching from the bar. He'd already changed out of his Pailin uniform and back into the Tigers World Series T-shirt he'd been wearing that morning, but he looked like he meant business.

"You *think*?" asked the woman, her voice somehow dripping with both sugar and evil. "Do your people not understand English, sweetie?"

Oh, what the—? I couldn't believe what I'd just heard. "I understand perfectly well," I said, trying unsuccessfully to keep the irritation out of my voice, "which is why I—"

Angry Lady #1 cut me off. "Well then, could you make us a replacement? In a pot that has never, ever touched raw meat?" She fussed with the silk scarf around her neck, and I briefly contemplated choking her with it.

"I'm so sorry," Nat cut in as he stepped up next to me. "The kitchen just closed." That was true. I'd sent Krai home as soon as he'd finished remaking the first curry, since he'd already stayed past the end of his shift.

"Then you should reopen it," the first woman said, crossing her arms and staring at me and Nat defiantly. "It's important that this dish be completely vegan. If there's any possibility that—"

"I'm sorry," I interrupted her, "but earlier you only specified vegetarian. You're drinking an iced tea with milk in it. So obviously you're not actually allergic—"

"It's not an allergy, sweetie, it's a preference," said the other woman. "But you know what, if you're going to be this difficult, just forget it. You won't be seeing us again."

"That's fine," I snapped. Nat elbowed me. I elbowed him right back. What was the point of trying to be nice if they were just going to leave anyway?

The two women started gathering their purses and coats, although not before sucking the very last dregs of iced tea from their straws. They threw down barely enough cash to cover the bill and headed toward the door, lecturing me the whole way. "It's a shame that your establishment doesn't value customer service. Or sensitivity to people's preferences. Or proper food preparation techniques." They were trading sentences, and their voices grew shriller with every word. "Rest assured we'll be contacting the Health Department about this. And we're telling all our friends to never come here!"

"Good. We don't want to see them either," I muttered under my breath, shutting the door as they swept through it and flipping the sign to CLOSED. I clicked the lock and turned around to find Nat shaking his head.

"Dude," he said.

"Dude," I agreed. I looked around the dining room, thought about the mess in the kitchen, relived the entire evening in my head, and suddenly felt very, very tired. "Hey," I said. "What if we went home right now and just did a double cleanup tomorrow night?"

"What, just leave it as is through both the lunch *and* dinner shifts? That's kind of gross," Nat pointed out. After a moment he added, "And I love it. Let's go." I grinned at him, grabbed our coats, and we left the restaurant right then.

I spent most of Monday morning totally high from the anticipation of getting to drive to school; my dad's Prizm was with my parents in D.C., but my mom's ancient red Corolla was all mine and Nat's while they were gone. Sarah seemed pretty amused by my giddiness, pointing out as she climbed into the passenger seat and buckled her seat belt, "It's not like you haven't driven before."

"Yeah," I said, slowly backing out of her driveway as her fat orange cat, Moxie, took her sweet time strolling out of the path of the wheels. "But I never got to drive *to school* before. I get to park in the lot today like everyone else with normal, non-paranoid parents."

"Yeah, but when Mom drops us off, we don't have to walk like, eight miles," Nat said from the backseat. An exaggeration, but he had a point—the student parking lot is huge, and if you don't get there at least half an hour before school starts, you end up stuck way out by the baseball diamond.

"Quit raining on my parade," I said, gleefully speeding up in order to pass a school bus.

"Just saying." He leaned up against the window and pulled his baseball cap down over his face to catch another five minutes of sleep.

"So if they're cool with you driving now, do you think they'll let you road-trip with me to Stanford this fall?" Sarah asked. "Curb check," she added, as I bumped the curb going around a corner. *Dammit*. I was never going to get good at driving if my parents didn't let me practice more often.

"Doubt it," I answered. "Unless a miracle happens in between now and then."

"You mean a miracle like both of us getting in and getting huge scholarships, and then they're so happy they let you do whatever you want for the rest of your life?" Sarah asked innocently.

I laughed. "Sure. Cross those fingers."

"Don't need to," she said. "It'll happen."

"Whatever you say, Pollyanna," I joked, pulling into the school parking lot and looking for a spot. It was slow going; tons of kids kept walking into our path, and there were exactly zero free spots that I could see. Yep, we were going to be stuck way the hell out there.

"The power of positive thinking!" Sarah said. "Oh my God, look!" Somebody pulled out of a space right by the door and I gunned into it.

"Wow," I said, putting the car in park.

"Wow," Nat echoed, opening his eyes and seeing where we were.

"Positive thinking," Sarah said cheerfully.

She flung open the door, got out of the car, and promptly tripped on the hem of her extra-long jeans.

We both cracked up.

After sixth period, I gave Sarah a ride home, told Nat that I'd pick him up after his Science Olympiad team practice, and then went to the restaurant to tally up the lunch receipts.

I unlocked the front door; the dining room was dark and quiet.

"Hello?" I called, walking back to the kitchen and pushing my way through the swinging doors. Krai was sitting on a stool by the prep table, waiting for me. He looked nervous; he was purposely unraveling the thread at the bottom hem of his sweatshirt, and he turned his baseball cap backward, then forward again, as I walked in.

"What?" I asked. Krai, not much for words, silently held out a hand-delivered envelope from "Richard R. Jenkins, Health Inspector."

Uh-oh.

"But—but we just—they inspected us like, five seconds ago!" I stammered. Okay, it was actually months ago, but I knew for certain that we weren't up for another inspection any time soon. "Why did you let them in?" I asked. "Never mind, obviously you had to let them in, but why did they show up?"

Krai shrugged. "I think a customer called to complain. They left that here when they were done," he said, pointing to the envelope that I was now nervously crunching in my hand.

"Oh, for crying out—" Those harpies from last night! I couldn't believe it! Man, they worked fast. I leaned against the edge of the prep counter with the Health Department envelope and opened it to scan the letter inside. It was probably just a warning notice. *Blah blah blah* inspection . . . *blah blah blah* complaint . . . *blah blah blah* violations . . . *blah blah blah* fines . . . *blah blah blah* thirty days . . . *blah blah blah* fifteen-day grace period . . . *blah blah*—wait, fines?

Uh-oh, indeed.

I took a deep breath and read the letter again, angling myself away from Krai so that he couldn't see it if he happened to glance over. Apparently, thanks to me blowing off the cleanup last night, the inspector had inspected us to the tune of $10,000 worth of violations. Ten grand due in six weeks. Oh my God. Oh my God, oh my God, oh my God. OhmyGodohmyGodohmyGod . . .

My hands shook as they held the letter, and I blinked like mad, trying to fight off tears as I walked out into the dining room and sank into a chair. Eight hundred for the food preparation surfaces not being properly sanitized. Three hundred for the freezer being two degrees too warm. Two hundred for the small trail of ants that had gathered where I hadn't mopped up some spilled ice cream thoroughly enough. Four hundred for a piece of raw chicken sitting a little too close to the onions. One hundred for one of our shelves being wood instead of metal—okay, that one wasn't my fault. But still . . . oh my God.

I nervously grabbed a handful of my own hair and twisted it, then kicked violently at the table leg closest to my right foot. *Why* had I chosen last night to skimp on the cleanup? *Why* hadn't I been nicer to those awful women despite their evilness? And *where* was I going to get $10,000? Because there was no way I was going to show my parents this letter. No. The restaurant meant too much to them. It was my family's entire source of income. Not to mention the trouble I was going to get in if they found out. They'd ship me off to Thailand, and I'd never get to go to Stanford. And even if they didn't ship me off, I wouldn't be able to go, because we wouldn't be able to afford it, because we couldn't afford a $10,000 fine. There was no way. We'd go out of business.

I blinked back more tears, then looked up at the ceiling and took a deep breath, followed by another. I pressed my hands, still cold from having been on the steering wheel a little while earlier, to my forehead, then put them down again, then folded the letter up and put it back in the envelope. No. I wasn't going to tell my parents. Or Krai, or my brother, or anyone else who might decide that the best course of action would be to 'fess up. No way. No how. This was my problem—this was my fault—and I was just going to have to fix it myself. I went back to the kitchen, where I smiled brightly at Krai and told him that the fine was minimal, that we'd pay it off with tonight's tip jar, and that he shouldn't worry about it. I then asked myself how the hell I was going to make ten grand in a month and a half.

Stripping?

No.

Prostitution?

No.

Selling my eggs to infertile couples who are really gung ho about having kids with smart DNA?

Maybe.

And then the solution dawned on me. And it was much, much worse.

chapter six

Ring. Ring. Ring. **It wasn't until later that night, after the** dinner shift, that I got up the courage to do what I had to do. Although the knowledge that the Health Department letter was in my backpack, probably burning a hole through the already-worn canvas, did help. I nervously scrunched myself into the fetal position on my bed, flipped a corner of the blanket over myself, and jiggled my cell phone impatiently, waiting for a pickup. Instead, I heard, "Hey, it's Camden. Leave a message, and maybe I'll call you back."

Argh! Fine, I'd talk to his voice mail. I had called once already, but had chickened out and hung up, so his phone was going to have two missed calls from me anyway. I wasn't about to make it three.

Beep. "Hey, Camden, it's Maya. Uh, your tutor. Or I guess, technically, your old tutor, although that was just—I mean, I just had a question for you, if you could give me a call back. Thanks. 'Bye." I started to close the phone, then remembered something and kept talking. "Oh, I got all your texts. Sorry I didn't answer them before. I guess this is me answering them now. Uh, 'bye." Yeah, I didn't sound like a douche bag or anything. It actually didn't matter, because he never called me back that night, even though I stayed up until one in the morning, and went to sleep with the phone right next to my head. Fine. It wasn't like I didn't know where his locker was.

"Hi!" I said brightly as Camden approached his locker the next morning, looking very sleepy; his hair was sticking up in all directions and he took several long blinks before registering who I was. "Can I talk to you about something?" My voice was as perky as I could possibly make it, even as I nervously clutched my books to my chest.

"Whatever," Camden said, having woken up enough to realize that I was standing right up against his locker door. He put a hand under each of my arms, picked me up without any apparent effort, and moved me aside, then started spinning his combination.

I forged ahead with my plan—if I didn't, I was going to lose my nerve. "Okay, so remember when you offered to pay me to do your homework for you?" I asked. The footsteps and chatter of people streaming past on their way to first period was noisy enough that I didn't bother to lower my voice. Nobody was paying attention anyway;

the ballots for Spring Fling King and Queen were going out this morning, and almost every conversation was some form of who to vote for, or why it was stupid to vote for anyone.

"Not really," Camden said, noisily transferring the contents of his book bag to his locker, except for his iPod nano, which he put in the back pocket of his jeans.

"You were in your hot tub," I said helpfully, then, remembering, blushed and started nervously twirling a piece of my hair.

Camden turned to me and smirked. "I'm in my hot tub a lot." He took off his coat and threw it in the locker as well, then shut the door and started off down the hallway.

I tagged along, steeling myself to the possibility of begging if necessary. "Well, anyway, you asked me, and I said no," I continued, trying to sound casual. "But I just wanted you to know that I changed my mind, and I'll totally do it now."

"Oh really?" he said, continuing to walk extremely fast. He gave Derek Rowe a casual punch in the shoulder as he passed us going in the opposite direction. Derek looked at us askance for a split second, obviously surprised to see us walking together, but he didn't slow down.

"Really," I said, quickly ducking in between some band kids in order to keep up with Camden, and earning myself a bonk on the elbow from one of their trumpet cases. Ow!

I had the cushioning of a cable-knit cardigan over a long-sleeved T-shirt, but that was still going to bruise.

"So you decided you couldn't resist me after all?" Camden asked. He turned to look down at me as he walked, a hint of a smile on his face.

"Yes," I said sarcastically, rolling my eyes, "that's exactly it. I could not get the image of your hotness out of my mind. All I could think about was how happy it would make me to add convenience to your life by doing your homework for you." Now that we were talking about it, I actually *was* having some problems getting rid of the mental image of him basically flashing me in his basement, but he didn't need to know that.

"Now you're talking," said Camden. I suppressed the urge to smack him upside the head. Seriously, I actually used my left hand to pin my right hand to the books I was carrying. Behind him, Leonard passed by us and waved energetically at me, before realizing who I was with. He stared at both of us suspiciously as he slowly moseyed away.

I waited until Leonard was out of hearing range, then asked Camden, "So, do we have a deal?"

"Nope," he said airily.

"What? Why not?"

"Too little, too late, sweetness. I already got another tutor." He paused outside of a classroom. "This is me," he said, indicating the door.

"You couldn't have gotten another tutor," I said, stopping with him. "The tutoring office said I was the only one qualified to teach Algebra II."

"Yeah, well, they sent me some kid," he shrugged. "Lenny somebody. Or Leo, maybe."

I cringed. "Leonard? The guy who just walked by us?"

"No idea. Little Asian kid? Glasses?"

"Yeah, but . . ." My mind searched frantically for a way to get around this unexpected turn of events. "Okay, well, if you just explain to the office that my quitting was a mix-up, then maybe they would let us—"

"Maybe," he said. "Maybe not." He flashed me a cocky smile. "Say please."

"Oh, for Christ's sake," I said.

He shrugged. "You're asking *me* for a favor, not the other way around."

I sighed. "Please?"

"How 'bout pretty please?" he asked.

"Pretty please," I said flatly, suppressing the urge to vomit.

"Pretty please with a really, really hot naked chick on top," he said.

I glared. He grinned. "Meet me in the parking lot after school and we'll talk," he said. He opened the door to his classroom and stepped inside. "And by the way?"

"What?" I asked.

"You're late for class." He slammed the door just as the bell started to ring.

"Hey," Sarah's voice called out, as I stood at my locker, jacket half-on, frantically throwing stuff into my backpack. Surprised, I jumped and spun around. It was the end of the day, and my state of controlled panic had turned into a state of *un*controlled panic. If Camden didn't come through for me when I met him in a few minutes, I was either going to be dead when my parents found out about the fine and killed me, or screwed when they found out and shipped me to Thailand. Either way, I'd be college education—less when the fine shut down the restaurant and took my family's livelihood and all our savings down with it. I felt sick to my stomach, and it took all my strength to greet Sarah back as if there were nothing, instead of *everything*, wrong.

"Hey!" I said. "Hi there! Hi. I mean, hey."

"Whoa, you okay?" Sarah asked, searching my face. Yep, I'd failed to conjure up an even remotely normal voice.

"Fine, fine," I lied, nervously chewing on my thumbnail. I fought the urge to spill the entire story to Sarah immediately. It wasn't like I didn't trust her. I knew she wouldn't tell, but she was also the type to encourage *me* to tell, and that was the last thing I wanted to do.

She raised her eyebrows and peered at me through her bangs. "So . . . you wanna go?" she asked.

I looked at her blankly.

"You said you'd give me a ride home before you went to work?"

"Huh?" I asked, pausing with my backpack halfway up on my shoulder. "Yes? No. Uh, I can't. Sorry, I—Nat texted me during sixth period, and apparently we both have to go straight there today. Like, literally now, because, you know . . ." I trailed off, hoping that she wouldn't notice that I had totally not given her a real reason.

"Oh, okay. No problem. Oh, I should probably run for the bus then!" Sarah started buttoning up her coat.

"Oh my God, yeah. Sorry, go!" I waved her in the general direction of the school doors.

"Going!" Sarah took off down the hall, trotting at first and then switching to a run, or at least as much of a run as she could handle given her giant book bag and clunky Mary Janes.

I yelled, "Sorry! Come by later and I'll give you free food!" to her retreating back, made a mental note to ask Krai to fry up some extra Shrimp Tod Mun (her favorite) in case she did stop by, and then practically sprinted to the parking lot to meet Camden. This time I made sure to stay far enough away from his car door that he couldn't lure me in and drive off someplace random; I was hovering about ten feet away from the Escalade's fender as he walked up.

"What are you doing," he asked, "standing far enough away so I can't lure you into the car and drive off someplace random?"

Observant bastard. "Just paranoid that your STDs have jumping skills," I said, covering. "So have you decided about this homework thing?"

"Sure," he said. "I've decided yes."

Yes!

"Except . . ."

No!

"I'd need to see a sample of the work first, you know." I stared at him. "What?" he asked. "That's standard business practice. Don't look so insulted." He threw the hood of his sweatshirt over his head and yanked the strings—it was beginning to drizzle a little.

"I don't see why I shouldn't," I said. "If you're rocking a D average right now, I'm pretty sure I could pump that up for you with both hands tied behind my back."

Apparently, somebody passing by only heard the last half of my sentence and started laughing uproariously. I stepped closer to Camden and lowered my voice. "Okay, so discussing cheating on homework for large sums of money probably isn't the smartest thing to do out in public," I muttered. He had to duck his head to hear me. "I have to be

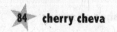

at work in like, two minutes, so just give me whatever you have for tonight, and I'll take care of it."

"Here," he said, reaching into his book bag and handing me his Algebra book and a ratty-looking assignment sheet. "But don't do too good a job, or else it won't be convincing."

"Duh," I said, examining the book. Either he or a previous owner had covered it with an impressive amount of graffiti, mostly doodles of transparent boxes and a couple of cartoon robots. "What do you usually get?" I asked.

"Zero out of ten," he answered cheerfully.

I rolled my eyes. "I'll aim for a four."

"Sweet."

"And then I can sort of gradually make it look like you're improving from week to week." I was getting ahead of myself, but I guessed I had to if I was planning on making any real money off of this little scheme.

"How soon can you have this done?" Camden asked.

I glanced at the assignment sheet and flipped his book to the right page to check out the problems. "I'll do it at work tonight."

"Cool. I'll come get it around eight."

"Only if you don't bring your friends." The last thing I needed was a replay of the other night.

"Free country. I can if I want," he said.

"Private restaurant. You can't if I don't want," I shot

back. He smiled good-naturedly as I crammed his stuff into my backpack, went over to my car, and headed to work.

It actually took me longer to do a convincingly bad job on Camden's quadratic equations than it would have taken me to do them right, especially since I tackled all my own homework first. I ended up having to stow his books underneath the bar as the dinner shift got under way, and I did the problems in between refilling water glasses and carrying plates of food. Luckily, Nat wasn't even remotely close to noticing that I was working out of a math book from a class I'd taken two years ago—he was too busy going over to Table Twelve every five minutes, where Star was camped out. She was sort of reading a book and sort of eating all the free food he kept on bringing over to her, but mostly she was exchanging flirty glances with him whenever his waiter duties landed him in her line of vision. Gross. Good for my little brother, I guess, but gross.

I was just putting the finishing touches on Camden's problem set by randomly changing some digits when the phone rang. "Hello, Pailin Thai Cuisine," I said.

"Hello, it's Mom. Everything okay? Any customers yet tonight?"

I looked around the restaurant. "Yeah, it's pretty good. A couple takeout calls, too."

"Are you and Nat okay? You're not scared to be staying in the house by yourself?"

I laughed. "No, we're not scared."

My mom chuckled as well. "Okay, okay. How's Krai? Dad talked to him last night and said he sounded stressed."

"What?" I sputtered, then closed my eyes and willed myself to remove the panic from my voice. I reached out and pressed the back of my hand to the side of a water pitcher, letting the cold from the ice calm me down a little.

"Why?" Deep breath. "Everything's fine," I said. "He's fine. It's just, you know, it's really busy because he has to cook everything himself, what with Dad being gone." Oh God. If Krai had told them about the letter yesterday even after I'd said it was nothing to worry about . . . if he'd gotten suspicious and said something . . .

"How's the trade show?" I asked, changing the subject.

"Oh, good." I heard my dad's muffled voice in the background, telling my mom something. "Oh," she added. "Dad says we might order some new silverware if we find some that's not too expensive, and there are lots of booths with free food samples."

"Oh, man. Nat would—"

"He would love that, I know. And of course, we love it too, because it's free." My mom chuckled to herself. "Okay, we'll call back later tonight. 'Bye."

"'Bye, Mom."

I hung up the phone and closed my eyes, breathing a sigh of relief. When I opened them, a party of four was standing in front of me, and I pasted a smile onto my face and kept it there for the rest of the evening. Right before closing—that is to say, nearly two hours after he said he would—Camden showed up to collect his homework, and I met him outside the restaurant before my brother could see what was going on. Again, not that he would have, since he and Star were now *both* camped out at Table Twelve, quizzing each other on the periodic table for Science Olympiad and looking like they were actually having a really fun time doing it.

"Here," I said, handing over the homework. "You'll probably want to copy it over in your own writing."

"Thanks," Camden said. He had a coat on over his hoodie now; it was a cold night and the drizzle from the afternoon had turned into straight-out rain. He folded the papers up and shoved them into his front pocket before they got too wet.

"Aren't you even going to look at it?" I asked, shivering a little; I'd come outside in just my waitressing outfit. "Wasn't that the point?"

He shrugged. "Yeah, well, I wouldn't know whether you'd done it right or not anyway."

"True," I said.

"But if we don't get caught, we're in business. Okay? Because I actually took a shot at doing my government essay just now, and, man . . . I would rather pay you to do it."

"Okay." I nodded and ducked back into the restaurant as he got into his car and drove off.

The next afternoon, between fifth and sixth periods, I found Camden standing by my locker with a hundred-dollar bill stuck to his forehead.

"We did it," he said, grinning, holding out his hand.

"*I* did it," I answered, shaking his hand.

"Same difference," he said, taking the money off his head and handing it to me. "Not that I was worried. I didn't even bother copying the whole thing you gave me and it still worked out. Now I can fire that Leonard kid and never go back to tutoring again. So, nice job." He impulsively hugged me, and I instinctively backed away.

"What?" he asked, looking down at me with a raised eyebrow.

"Nothing," I said. My face began to redden, although I wasn't sure why. It might have had something to do with the fact that I'd just noticed that his blue eyes exactly matched the color of his shirt.

Camden looked at me with interest. "Paranoid 'cause you got a boyfriend or something?" He looked me up and down like he had when we'd first met the week before, but for some reason it felt different this time.

"No." My face was completely red now, and I started slowly inching away from him.

"Have you *ever* had a boyfriend?" His tone was curious, not judgmental, but it still made me nervous.

"Uh . . ." I started toying with my hair. I don't know why I didn't just tell him no—there's no shame in never having had a boyfriend. Right?

"Huh. Have you ever even kissed anybody?"

"Uh . . ." I looked away from him, at the lockers, at the STUDENT CAR WASH! posters in the hallway, at someone's backpack as it passed through my line of vision, at anything. Camden studied me for a moment. Then he took a step forward, bent his head, and gently kissed me.

"Now you have," he said.

And after smiling and handing me two books, he walked away.

Oh. My. God.

I suddenly realized that several people in the hallway were staring—some quizzically, some bemusedly, this one chick rather jealously—so I ducked into an empty classroom and shut the door. Everything I was holding tumbled to the floor as I leaned against the wall and pressed my hands to my forehead. What had just happened? Ew! Ew! Except . . . not ew? Except . . . eeewww! He—I—we—*what?*

My first kiss—not something I'd pondered *that* much, but certainly something I'd imagined—had come out of nowhere.

And it had been with *Camden King*, of all people.

Which was disgusting.

Or maybe not.

I sank to the floor, pulling my knees up to my chin, then glanced down and looked at the books Camden had given me. It was another Algebra assignment and a Chemistry problem set, with a Post-it note stuck on·top that read, *$200*. A quick mental calculation told me that after this assignment, I would be three percent of the way to my $10,000 goal. Great. Awesome. Not nearly fast enough, but it was a start. I'd earn the money, pay the fine, save the restaurant, and save my college fund. No problem.

It was doable. It was totally doable.

I thought about Camden kissing me and felt my face go red again.

It was just going to be a little more complicated than I'd thought.

chapter seven

I had two things to hide from my parents that evening when they got back: the fine, and the fact that I had now been kissed. The second one would be effortless; lying by omission in order to avoid being yelled at was not really a new thing for me. In fact, it dated all the way back to when I was eight and the toilet had overflowed, and I'd opted not to tell them that I'd thrown half a nectarine in there to see what would happen. But the first one . . .

"Whoa, you got the mail? How'd you get the mail? You never get the mail. You don't even have a key." I practically tackled Nat, who was standing outside our restaurant mailbox with several envelopes and a catalog in his hand. It was shortly before we were due to start work for the evening—our last kickoff of the dinner shift by ourselves before our parents got back. He raised an eyebrow as I snatched the mail away from him.

"I got here just as the mailman was leaving," he said, lazily leaning back against the wall.

"Oh, hahaha, you guys got here at the same time. What a crazy coincidence, huh? Tiny world," I said, rapidly flipping through the pile of envelopes. Bills . . . junk mail . . . nothing from the Health Department. I mentally high-fived myself—it was highly unlikely that they would send another notice only two days after leaving the first one, but I wasn't taking any chances.

"You order something?" Nat asked.

"What?"

"What are you waiting for? It's still like, a full month before you find out from Stanford, isn't it?" Nat propelled himself off the wall and into an upright position, then noticed his shoelace was untied and bent over to fix it.

"Oh! Oh, right. Yeah. I, uh, I thought it was April already," I said lamely.

Nat looked at me weirdly. "Okay, I know we joke about this, but are you actually doing drugs? Because if you are, I might have to say something to Mom and Dad about it."

"Yes," I said. "I'm a crack addict. It's a cry for help. Please tell our parents before I hurt them and myself."

He looked at me for a second and then laughed. *Phew.* I followed him as he stood up and went around the corner to the restaurant door. He opened it for me as we both walked in and started hitting light switches and straightening place mats, as usual. Since it was Wednesday, the dinner shift was pretty dead; only a handful of tables over a span of three hours. Soon after, my parents got back, with very little fanfare, their car rolling slowly past the front window before turning the corner into their usual parking spot. I saw them come in the door from my post at the cash register, both of them looking weary from their ten-hour trip and a little damp from the never-ending spring rain. I caught my mom's eye, waving with my left hand as I cradled the phone on my shoulder and took down a takeout order with my right. She waved back and smiled as she and Dad both looked around to see customers eating, Nat refilling water, everything calm and smooth and under control. They both beamed. Yes!

"Everything good?" Mom asked, coming around behind the bar and dropping her bag on the floor. I nodded as Dad patted me on the head and Nat on the shoulder, then unbuttoned his coat and headed back toward the kitchen.

"Chocolate," Mom said, handing me a cute little boxed favor from the wedding. I opened it up and crammed both pieces—it was chocolate-covered dried mango—into my mouth right away. Nat devoured his as well, and as my dad disappeared through the swinging kitchen doors, I crossed

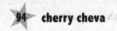

my fingers that everything in there was going as well as it was out here.

"Maya," Dad's voice called out from behind the kitchen door a few moments later. I couldn't tell if his tone was angry or not.

"Yeah?" I squeaked. I looked at my mom, who was now sitting with her accounting book and reading glasses as if she'd never left, and she nodded permission for me to leave the phone. I walked back toward the swinging kitchen doors and poked my head through.

"Yeah, Dad?" I looked at him nervously. He was wearing his Michigan baseball cap again and, like my mom, seemed like he'd totally been there for the past five days.

"Please remind me to get a new metal shelf," Dad said. I caught my breath. Was he psychic? Did he know about that part of the fine? "This wood one looks like it is about to break," he continued, jiggling it to demonstrate how wobbly the little legs at the bottom were. A can of bamboo shoots rolled off of it, and he caught it in his hand.

"Nice catch," I said.

Then I waited.

My dad smiled and put the bamboo can back on the shelf, but didn't say anything else. I waited a little longer. If he were somehow psychic and had managed to figure out that our wonky wooden shelf was just one tiny part of the much bigger problem I'd created while they were out of town—but no. Dad gave the shelf one last experimental tap, then moved on to checking out what Krai was stir-frying on the stove. Okay. He didn't suspect anything. Guilt was clearly making me paranoid.

"Okay!" I said brightly, finally responding to his request. "Don't worry. I'll remind you."

"Thank you," he said. He ruffled my hair and stepped inside the fridge to do a supply check. I collapsed against the wall in relief.

"You asleep again?" asked Nat.

I stood up straight and made a face at him. "Nope, just glad they're back," I said. "Now I can go back to being irresponsible." Nat grinned and piled a rice bowl, a plate of Pad Thai, and a bowl of Masamun Curry onto a tray, and we both walked back through the swinging doors to the dining room. I looked around. My mom was cheerful. My dad was cheerful. Krai hadn't said anything about the health inspection, and the restaurant was under control. Everything was awesome.

A party of twelve walked in and my mom sat them in my section. *Ugh.*

"She works hard for the money!" my brother sing-songed in my ear.

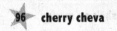

A party of eight walked in and my mom sat them in his section.

"So does he," I said back to him.

That night, I barely slept, what with finishing my own homework, and Camden's, and reliving the whole kissing thing over and over again in my head, no matter what I did to get my mind off of it. My hours of unconsciousness totaled three—most of which I spent having nightmares about giving grisly birth to a half-Asian daughter who, in addition to being a spoiled brat and a colossal slut, would, when she grew up, set a bunch of roaches free in my parents' restaurant and then get on a massive citywide P.A. system to announce to the world that the blame should be laid on her mom—me. The next day, I pondered skipping school, but I figured that now was not the time to start messing with my perfect attendance record. Besides, that fine wasn't going anywhere; if I was going to keep making money off of Camden, I was just going to have to deal with whatever consequences yesterday's kiss wanted to throw my way. Step one of dealing: Pretend it never happened.

"Hey, hot lips."

Or not.

"Morning," I said, in what I hoped was a perfectly neutral tone of voice. We had only a few minutes before the first-period bell rang, but I waited until Camden moved off of my locker door of his own accord instead of shoving him out of the way so I wouldn't have to touch him. Then I fished his homework assignments out of my backpack as quickly as possible and held them out to him with two fingers.

"These are done," I said.

"Cool." He took the papers. He was wearing a slouchy gray long-sleeved T-shirt and dark blue cords—an outfit that coordinated just a little too well with my own gray sweater and dark jeans combo. Coincidence, of course, but yuck.

"So . . . that's two hundred," I said, deliberately moving away from him.

"Sweet," he said. He reached into his wallet and started to hand me some cash, and then stopped. "Wait. Don't I get a discount?"

"What do you mean?" I asked.

"The hookup discount," he said, smirking.

"Don't you mean the hookup *bonus* for me for having to suffer through that?" I shot back. If he wasn't going to let me ignore it, I sure wasn't gonna pretend I enjoyed it.

"Oh, please," said Camden. "You so wanted it." He edged toward me.

"I *so* did not," I said, growing more furious by the moment. I snatched the cash out of his hand and pocketed it.

"Liar," he said. "That was the best three seconds of your life so far." He was now leaning in close to me, and I could see the edge of his cell phone sticking out of his pants pocket.

"Wrong," I answered. "*This* is the best three seconds of my life so far." In one quick motion, I grabbed his cell out of his pocket, threw it in my locker, slammed the door shut, and walked away.

"Do you have something to tell me?" Cat demanded later that morning in English, as soon as I sat down next to her.

"You're having a bad hair day," I offered.

"Bitch," she said, pulling her battered camouflage hoodie up over her unruly waves without missing a beat. She lowered her voice. "No. Do you have something to tell me about a certain Camden King?"

Christ. Had she heard?

"What about him?" Sarah asked, sliding into the seat behind me. At the front of the classroom, Ms. Flannery started energetically writing the words TROILUS AND CRES-SIDA on the board. She screwed up the spelling on *Cressida* and went with *Cresida* and *Cresseda* before going back to her original. Then she finally noticed that she'd written the entire thing on a slant, erased it, and started all over.

"Nothing about him," I said lightly, casually flipping my hair over my shoulder. "I'm his tutor, he's annoying, that's pretty much the end of that story." I made a big show of opening up my notebook and taking out a pen, in order to start copying down what Ms. Flannery was writing, but before I even put the point to paper, Cat reached over, took the pen out of my hand, and seamlessly passed it to Sarah, who held it out of my reach. Damn them.

"Really?" Cat said. "Because I heard you made out with him in the hallway yesterday."

"What?" Sarah screeched.

Ms. Flannery, who had just written, 10 PAGES, DUE MONDAY, on the board, turned around and said, "You're seniors, this is A.P., ten pages is nothing, and yell that loud again and you're getting detention." She turned back to the board. Sarah blushed bright red and ducked so that her hair fell into her face, then switched to writing in her notebook, which she shoved at me.

WHAT??? she wrote.

I desperately wanted to tell her the truth. My first kiss, despite the insanely sketchy circumstances surrounding it, was something I'd always envisioned sharing with her right away. But I knew that if I did, I'd end up spilling the stuff about the homework cheating as well, which she would undoubtedly be less understanding about. *Nothing,* I scribbled back. *Just a rumor.*

Cat leaned in and interjected with her spidery handwriting. *I heard it from like, 4 different people.*

Well, they heard wrong!!!! I wrote. *Because GROSS!!!*

No kidding, wrote Sarah. *Plus, that would be sooo shady cuz I heard he just asked Dani Davis to the Spring Fling.*

I stared at what she'd written for a moment. Camden asked Dani to—but they weren't even dating! If they were dating, everyone at school would know; they'd been together for a month or so our sophomore year, and it had been big news when they broke up. Wait, if he was dating Dani again, why would he kiss me? Maybe they were just going to the dance as friends? Maybe they *were* dating and he was totally cheating on her? Maybe they *were* dating but had an open relationship? Maybe they *weren't* dating, but he wanted to be, so he was using me to make her jealous?

Forget it. I shook my head. I had to stop thinking about it.

Good! They deserve each other, I wrote in Sarah's notebook. I nudged it back toward her, and she and Cat both leaned over to read it.

Totally, Sarah wrote, and then drew a smiley face.

You better not be lying, slut, wrote Cat. But she followed it up with a smiley as well.

We couldn't have continued our back-and-forth anyway, because as soon as the bell rang, Ms. Flannery asked Cat what she thought of Pandarus's role in Troilus and

Cressida's affair. Cat's answer of "He was a pimp" got a laugh from the class, even though she was actually being dead serious, so I was saved by the teacher . . . for now.

Of course, if my friends, who weren't exactly in the loop at our school, had already heard rumors, there were bound to be more. I don't know who I'd been kidding, thinking I could pretend nothing had ever happened. Several people in the hallway had seen me and Camden kiss for at least a split second, and while most people didn't know who I was, *everybody* knew who he was. Plus, there was apparently the Dani drama in the mix as well, making him even more of a man-slut than I'd thought. He'd probably just kissed me to mess with my head. Well, I wasn't going to let him. I was going to get past this as quickly as humanly possible. As the tabloid hoes like Lindsay Lohan lived, so would I—I'd been caught doing something I was ashamed of, and now I had to deny, deny, deny.

Which I ended up doing a lot of at lunch.

"Oh my God, Maya! Did you kiss Camden King in the hallway yesterday?"

"No, of course not."

"Hey, are you Maya? Did you really make out with C.K. yesterday?"

"Nope."

"Hey, you're that nerdy chick who somehow got Camden King to feel her up, right?"

"What? Ew, no!"

"Hey, you! Asian girl. Camden King said he nailed you."

Okay, that was it.

After school, I walked right up to Camden at his locker and smacked him upside the head. He didn't even flinch, just turned and glared down at me. "What's *your* problem?"

I crossed my arms and glared right back up at him. "Are you starting rumors that you had sex with me?"

"What? Why would I do that?" He rolled his eyes at me dismissively. "You're hot, but you're a total dork."

I blushed with a mixture of embarrassment and anger. What the hell kind of a compliment was that? What the hell kind of an *insult* was that? "So how come people have been coming up and asking me about you all day?" I demanded.

"Dude, how should I know?" A text beep told him that his cell phone was now in the outside pocket of my backpack, so he reached over my shoulder, unzipped the zipper, and got it back. I didn't bother stopping him; it wasn't like I'd been planning on keeping the thing. "You know this school," he continued, scrolling through all the texts and calls he'd missed all day while he was phone-less. "People like to make a big deal out of nothing."

"Yeah, well—" I stopped. Wait, us kissing was *nothing*? Fine. I mean, of course it was. He was right. Duh.

"Yeah, well," I said again, "the last thing I need is for

half the world to be convinced you gave me herpes, so if you could do me a favor and just deny everything if anyone asks you—"

"You sure?" Camden asked, looking up from his phone. "You'd probably be a lot more popular if people thought you hooked up with me."

"A risk I'm willing to take," I said flatly.

"Fine. I'll deny that I hooked up with the crazy Kabbalah girl." He flicked at the white string bracelet on my right wrist.

"Those bracelets are red. This is a *sai sin* I got from a Buddhist monk," I said. "It's for good luck."

"Yeah? How's that working out for you so far?"

"Well, lately? Not so great." I glared at him again.

He sighed. "Okay. Fine. Are you done flipping out? Can we get down to business already?"

Right. Business. $9,700 to go.

"Yeah," I said, my shoulders sinking a little. "Whatcha got?"

"Algebra, some Government crap, and this Chemistry problem set and lab, although the lab's not due until Monday. . . ." He piled a bunch of books into my arms. "And Dani's got the same Algebra, plus—"

"Wait a minute. What?" I stepped away from him so that he couldn't hand me anything else and quickly glanced around. The hallway was emptying out; kids with only six periods had taken off for the day, kids with seven were due in class in—the bell rang—zero seconds. It was safe to talk, but I motioned for Camden to lower his voice anyway.

"Dani Davis," he repeated, quieter. "She's in my Algebra class. She's got the same problem set as me."

"Yeah, I know who she is," I said impatiently, "but since when am I doing her work too?"

"Since I told her this morning how awesome you are at it, and she wants in."

"You told her? Are you crazy? You can't tell other people! She's the principal's daughter—we're gonna get caught!" I stared at him in disbelief.

"No, we're not," he said smoothly. "We haven't so far."

"It's been two days!" I exclaimed.

"Well, were you suddenly planning on doing something different or stupid?"

"No," I said.

"Okay, then that means we're going to continue to not get caught." He put another book on top of the pile I was holding.

"What if *Dani* does something different or stupid?" I asked.

"She won't. She's awesome," said Camden.

"She's got the words *Easy Rider* tattooed on her lower back," I said.

"That's after the pony she got for her tenth birthday present."

"That's even *more* disturbing."

"Look, Dani's totally cool. She's one of my best friends, okay?"

I quashed the urge to ask him if by "best friend," he meant "girlfriend."

Camden continued. "She's not gonna tell. So come on, do us both a favor? And yourself?" He waved Dani's assignment sheets in front of me. I sighed and nodded. "Great," he said, plunking all of her stuff into my arms, as I struggled not to wilt under the weight. "She'll pay the same," he said, "even though technically, since it's the same questions, I feel like we should work out some sort of a deal—"

"No deal," I said quickly. "I have to do hers differently than yours anyway, or else we'd get caught. Hundred bucks or forget it."

"You drive a hard bargain," Camden said.

"I drive lots of hard things," I snapped. Wait a minute.

Camden laughed appreciatively. "Well, quit being so paranoid about getting caught, and we'll be golden," he said.

"Sorry, but being suspended isn't that high on my list of priorities," I said.

"I've been suspended four times," he said cheerfully.

"Being like you isn't one of my priorities either," I

pointed out. He just grinned and handed me even more books.

"And here's Stacey's stuff," he said. He topped the pile off with a sparkly purple notebook. *Stacey Ray* was written on it in Day-Glo pink puff pen.

"Oh my God, how many people have you told?" I asked. The purple notebook started sliding off the top of the pile, and I tilted back ever so slightly to save it from falling.

"Just them," Camden said. "But hey, keep up the good work and maybe this turns into something." He patted me on the head condescendingly, which I couldn't do anything about because of all the books I was holding, and then he sauntered off, grabbing his car keys out of his pocket with one hand while flipping open his phone and starting to send a text with the other. I leaned against the row of lockers for a moment, struggling with all the weight, then sank to the floor and started piling the books up in stacks. *Yeesh.* Tonight was looking ugly, although lucrative. The first thing would have to be my own homework, of course; I had some extra-credit English questions due tomorrow for a book that I had yet to read, although at least *The Turn of the Screw* only had ninety-six pages. I also had my Physics problem set, my French mini comp (only half a page), and my history reading (just one chapter). Thus far, doable. Then there was Camden's work: Algebra (a breeze), plus

Government and Chemistry, which would hopefully be easy since I'd taken A.P. Chem the year before. There was Dani's, too: Algebra, Government, history. And finally, Stacey's: Government, Chemistry, and Spanish.

I've never taken a day of Spanish in my life.

El crap.

chapter eight

It turns out, doing one homework assignment badly in fifteen minutes is pretty easy. Doing three of them in a row is harder. Doing eight of them in a row is *exponentially* harder. I didn't sleep much—big surprise—which led me to screw up most of the lines in my half of the French dialogue I was assigned to do with Priti Radatha the next day, leading Simone (she told us that if anyone of us ever called her Madame Lipschitz, she'd flunk us instantly) to ask me, "*Que s'est produit?*" and me to answer, "Huh?" as she shook her head and wrote in a B– next to my name in her grade book.

I got a check minus on my physics problem set as well, which, being just a problem set, wasn't going to hurt my grade much, but it wasn't going to help it, either. *Ouch.* Hopefully, whatever damage I was doing to my own G.P.A. could be repaired once I paid off the fine, or else my merit scholarship chances would be headed down the drain, and I could kiss Stanford good-bye even if I did get in.

Plus, at lunch I had a pissed-off Stacey Ray to deal with.

"You didn't do my Spanish!" she whined, after accosting me in the hallway on my way to the bathroom. She yanked on my sleeve and pouted, tottering in her four-inch purple wedge heels. I could feel her shimmery beige fingernails pressing through the fabric and into my skin.

"Shhh!" I said, yanking her through the door. I eyed all the stalls suspiciously and ducked my head under to make sure they were feet-free, but luckily nobody else was in there. "I didn't have your number, but I told Camden to tell you that I don't take Spanish and couldn't do it," I said, backing up against the door in case somebody tried to open it. "Didn't he tell you?"

"No," she said, turning to the mirror to check out her hair. "Maybe," she added. "I don't remember." She started taking individual ringlets of her hair and curling them around her fingers; the drizzle had turned to rain again today, giving the air enough humidity to make her usually perfect blond coif frizz ever so slightly. She yanked on one ringlet and watched, pleased, as it bounced, just like in a shampoo commercial.

I sighed. "Anyway, if you knew I wasn't going to do it, would you have actually done it?" I asked her.

"No," she answered, then looked a little confused.

"So . . . no loss there," I pointed out.

"I guess," she said hesitantly, taking a bulging makeup bag out of her purse and setting it on the edge of the sink. She started rifling through it; I counted six lip glosses and four eye shadows in the outside pocket alone.

"And it's not like I'm still charging you for it. I'm not," I said, continuing to try and defuse her irritation.

"Oh my God, you're right!" Stacey's face lit up, and she swiveled around to look at me. "I just made a hundred bucks!"

"Sure, if you want to think of it that way." I shrugged.

"That's so awesome!" she said. She picked up a mascara tube and pointed it at me excitedly.

"I know!" I agreed. Her enthusiasm was actually kind of infectious.

Stacey smiled widely, anger thoroughly forgotten, then rifled through her makeup bag again and turned to the mirror to reapply her Lip Venom. "Ow," she said as she put it on. "Ow. Ow. Ow."

"Why do you wear that stuff if it hurts?" I asked.

"Because when boys see big, luscious lips, they think of—"

I left the bathroom to avoid hearing the rest of her sentence.

For the next three days, every free moment of which I spent doing other people's homework, my mantra was "Sleep is for the weak. Sleep is overrated. Screw sleep." After the small Spanish gaffe with Stacey, I'd made sure to tell Camden that he had to vet everyone's assignment requests beforehand, because I enjoyed calling his pals if something went wrong about as much as they enjoyed getting calls from me. My weird pseudo-bonding session with Stacey in the bathroom apparently did not carry over to the rest of our lives, as the next several times I passed her in the hallway, she ignored me as usual. I tried to make eye contact once or twice, figuring I should at least try to be friendly, but after a few unsuccessful tries I started ignoring her as usual again too.

Granted, I was now $1,400 richer, but I was also the owner of some very large under-eye circles. Maybe it was time to explore concealer. It was *certainly* time to start figuring out where I was gonna get more money, because at the rate I was going—even with doing Camden's, Dani's, *and* Stacey's work—I was never going to get to my $10,000 goal in time.

The popular kids seemed to have developed psychic powers and sensed this. A few days into my triple-strength homework nightmare, I was trudging down the hallway after the welcome ring of the end-of-sixth-period bell, vaguely pondering whether "SexyBack" or "Buttons" would be a better song with which to make my strip joint Amateur

Night debut—if it came to that—when I found a bunch of them waiting by my locker: Camden, Dani, Stacey, Brad, and Derek. What the—?

"Hey," Camden said as I walked up, giving me sort of a half wave. The rest of them just stood there, except for Dani, who gave my sweatshirt and jeans outfit a once-over, and then looked thoughtful as she toyed with a piece of her dark, flatironed hair.

"Hey," I said cautiously.

"Hey," said everybody else. I glanced at all of them, not bothering to hide my weirded-out expression at the fact that like, half the Spring Fling court was surrounding my locker, and asked, "What's going on?"

"Got some more customers for ya," said Camden, taking off his baseball cap to bend the brim, and then putting it back on again.

"Wait, she deals drugs too?" asked Brad. I couldn't tell if he was serious or not. Apparently, neither could the student teacher passing by us in the hallway; she whipped her head around to stare suspiciously for a moment before either deciding that we were harmless or deciding to stroll on over to Principal Davis's office in an exceedingly casual manner. Dani and Derek both noticed her paranoid expression; Dani giggled and Derek smirked.

"Oh my God, Camden. Can I talk to you alone for a second?" I took his sleeve and pulled him a few feet away to the little side hall where the Chem lab was. Dani and Derek both continued to smirk as we disappeared out of their line of vision. Stacey and Brad probably would've been smiling too, if they hadn't spontaneously started making out against a TRY OUT FOR THE TALENT SHOW! NO TALENT NECESSARY! poster.

Camden disengaged my fingers from his sleeve, then wandered into the empty Chem lab and sat down on one of the tables, swinging his long legs over the chair in front of him. I followed him and paused in the doorway so I could keep a lookout if necessary.

"Okay, seriously," I said, my voice low. "How suspicious does this look? Why are you congregating everyone around my locker?" I glanced behind me. There was nobody there.

"It's a school hallway, and we're students standing in it. What's suspicious about that?" Camden stretched his arms over his head and then turned so that he could lie back on the table. He put his hands under his head and stared up at the ceiling.

"Nothing, until one of your idiot friends says something too loudly," I hissed. "It's not like we're talking in code about this stuff. Someone—everyone—could totally hear!"

Out in the main hallway, I heard Brad yelp and say in a disgusted voice, "Jesus, Stace, are you wearing that sulfuric acid stuff on your mouth again?" *Heh.*

"You're so paranoid," Camden said, yawning. "Remind me never to let you try weed."

I crossed my arms and didn't say anything, just stared at him.

Camden moved back to a sitting position and shrugged. "Look, Derek and Brad want in now too."

"No way," I said instantly. "The more people who know, the more likely we are to get in trouble."

"Come on," Camden wheedled. "Didn't we already decide that train of logic doesn't work?"

"No, you decided that," I said. But . . . did he have a point? It *was* only a month or so that I would need to do this; and if I didn't manage to pay off the fine in time, there wouldn't be any point in continuing anyway. Maybe the odds of getting caught weren't too bad. Maybe I could make it to ten grand and then just quit the whole shebang before any teachers were the wiser. They couldn't really punish me if it was already over with by the time they figured it out, right? I started calculating in my head how much I could earn doing five people's homework at an average rate of twelve assignments per week. Five times twelve was sixty, times—wait, five times a hundred was—wait, twelve times . . . I suddenly realized that I couldn't do the math. I couldn't even do simple multiplication. Because my brain was fried. Because I was too sleepy. Because I'd been doing three people's homework in addition my own for the past several days.

"I'm not sure I have the time," I said wearily, and then instantly regretted it. I couldn't stop now, could I? What mattered more—my sanity, or paying off the fine? I had been leaning toward sanity, but maybe that was the insanity talking.

"Aw, man! Seriously?" Camden looked bummed.

"Camden. Look at my face," I said.

He trained his blue eyes on me and looked. "What about it?"

"I have giant dark circles under my eyes!" I exclaimed.

"Can't see 'em," he said, smiling. "Maybe I should look closer." He got up and walked over to the doorway where I was standing, then playfully started leaning his face right into mine. I started to back away, and then all of a sudden, I heard Cat's voice behind me in the hallway.

"What's up, Maya?" she asked, her voice dripping with innocence. I spun around and saw Cat, Sarah, and Jonny all standing there.

"Oh, hey," I said, springing away from Camden. "Uh . . . I was just . . . do you guys know Camden?" My lame cover-up attempt, and then my lame introduction in order to cover up the lame cover-up attempt, didn't matter—Camden had gone past me through the doorway and taken off. I peeked around the corner into the main hall, back toward my locker, only to see him and his friends disappearing in the direction of the exit to the student parking lot.

"We're headed over to the tutoring office and wanted to see if you were coming," Cat said as we walked back toward my locker. "What the hell's all that?" she asked.

Camden, Stacey, and Dani had left a big pile of books on the floor by my locker door, along with a Post-it note covered with scribbled numbers and assignments. I quickly dropped my backpack and jacket on top of the stack to try to cover it up before they could see what it was.

"Nothing," I said, opening my locker as quickly as I could and shoving all the stuff inside.

"And why were you hanging out with that guy?" she continued.

"Are you trying to get closer to Derek again or something?" Sarah teased.

Jonny turned to her, mouth agape. "She used to like him?" he asked.

"Fifth grade," she answered, giggling. "Before you got here."

"Man, I missed out on everything," he said, shaking his head.

"Not anymore," Cat said cheerfully, before fixing an appraising gaze back on me.

"I wasn't hanging out with him," I said defensively. "I'm tutoring Camden—"

"But you're never in the office anymore," Sarah said

gently. There wasn't a smidge of accusation in her voice, but somehow, it still seemed like one.

"True. We're never in the office because he takes offense to it for some reason, so we always end up going someplace else," I said rapidly. "And whatever, we were just figuring out the next time we're going to have a session. So, yeah." Wow. Not only was I lying to my parents, but now I was lying to my friends, as well. And the ease with which I was spewing completely untrue statements was beginning to scare me. I was a great person. I was a really upstanding citizen.

"Well, I hope you didn't have to talk to him for long," Sarah said, making a face at the thought. She blew a puff of air upward to get her bangs out of her eyes. "He and his friends are just a bunch of jerks."

"Yeah," said Cat. "I think half my brain cells die if I come within ten feet of that Brad guy."

"Stacey Ray has huge boobs," Jonny said cheerfully. We all looked at him. "What?" he asked. "I'm allowed to state facts if I want."

"Jonny's oversexed," Cat said instantly.

"Jonny's a tool," I added.

"Jonny's a dork," Sarah said at almost exactly the same time.

"See? You guys are allowed to state facts too." He grinned at us. "So, I take it you're not coming, Maya?" He tilted his head down the hallway in the direction of the tutoring office.

"No," I said. "I'm . . . I'm just gonna meet Camden at Starbucks later."

"All right, slut," Cat said cheerfully, as Jonny matter-of-factly started pushing her down the hallway.

"Okay," Sarah said, eyeing me curiously as she started to follow them. "IM me later if you wanna trade history notes."

"Sure, absolutely," I said, guiltily avoiding her eyes. The three of them wandered off, and I waited until they were out of sight before heading toward the public bus stop to catch my usual ride to work. Too bad I was halfway there before I realized that I'd forgotten Camden's and everyone else's books in my locker. *Argh!* I sprinted back to school to get them, but by the time I got back outside, it was clearly too late. I had to wait for the next bus, shivering in the dreary drizzle, which meant there was no way in hell I was getting to work on time. It figured, with the way the rest of the day had been going.

When the bus finally got to my stop, I jumped off and practically sprinted into the restaurant, throwing my backpack on the floor behind the bar. I tore off my jacket, grabbed a Pailin shirt, and changed right there instead of going into the bathroom.

"Maya!" my mom said. She took off her reading glasses and glared at me.

"What? I'm late, I know. I'm sorry!" I said. Next to my

mom was a giant stack of freshly laundered napkins that Nat and I were supposed to have had folded before the shift started; Nat had gotten there before me and had folded about twenty or so (he was glaring at me from his seat at the bar), but clearly they'd both been waiting for me to help. I rushed back out to the other side of the bar, tripping over my backpack on the floor in the process, and grabbed a stool to sit down next to him. I took a foot-high stack of napkins and started folding them into our usual elaborate stand-up shape as quickly as I could.

"Did you get the mail?" Mom asked.

Dammit!

"No, I forgot. I'm sorry. I'll go grab it!" I started to get up.

"No, it's okay. I can do it," said my mom. She punched a few buttons on the cash register, made a note to herself, and got up.

"No, I can do it." I was standing now.

"You fold, I get mail," she said, coming out from behind the bar and gently pushing me back down onto the stool. She grabbed her ring of keys and headed for the door.

Oh God.

Obviously, the chances of there being another letter from the Health Department were low. The deadline was still over a month away, so it wasn't like they had to send a reminder notice. But I wasn't sure. So I was terrified.

I watched my mom go out the front door and disappear around the corner. Okay. I told myself that I shouldn't panic, nonetheless folding a napkin completely wrong as I started to panic. The odds were with me. The odds were with me. The odds were with me. . . .

My mom came back around the corner, shuffling through the mail. She paused on one envelope and my heart stopped . . . then she started shuffling again. She paused on another and I had another mini cardiac arrest . . . then she moved on to the next one, as she came through the door and back into the restaurant.

"Anything for me?" I asked brightly. My hands were shaking. I violently clutched one of the napkins I was folding to try and hide my nerves.

"Catalog," my mom said, handing me a J.Crew catalog. I've never actually bought anything from there in my life— way too expensive, even the sale stuff most of the time—but I like to look. She put the rest of the mail on the bar next to the reservations book, and I tried my best to look casual as I reached over and flipped through the stack. Bills, junk mail, more bills . . . and nothing from the Health Department. *Phew.* That was too close. Waaay too close. It took me a second to realize that my eyes were filling up with tears, and suddenly my mom was looking at me with concern.

"Are you okay?" she asked, putting her hands on my cheeks and gently brushing my hair out of my face.

"Fine," I said. "Just a little stressed out." I blinked and looked up at the ceiling as she patted my hand sympathetically. *Don't cry*, I told myself. *Everything's fine. Don't cry. Don't cry.*

And I didn't . . . at least not then.

That night was a late one at the restaurant; in spite of the rain, which had been steadily elevating over the last few hours from a drizzle to a full storm, or perhaps because of it, the last customer didn't leave until ten thirty. And thanks to the vacuum cleaner breaking down right when we needed it the most—a pair of unruly toddlers had been so kind as to accidentally-on-purpose smash one of our glass candleholders, scattering glittery, dangerous shards all over the carpet beneath Table Nine—my entire family didn't get home until well past eleven.

Nat got out of the car, went right up to his room, and passed out, and if all I'd needed to do was to finish up my own homework, I could've done the same shortly thereafter. But no, I had three other people's work to do as well. *Sigh.* I leaned back against the inside of my closed bedroom door and looked around my room: at the books piled up in every corner; at the dozens of multicolored Post-it notes I'd been using to keep track of other people's homework logistics; at the little flash drive that I'd been shuttling all the typed assignments around on, sitting forlornly by itself in the middle of the worn carpet . . . and suddenly, the tears started.

I threw myself onto my bed and shoved my face into my pillow, covering my head with my comforter and hoping that my parents couldn't hear. I sobbed, exhausted from lack of sleep, exhausted from being plagued with either panic or guilt twenty-four hours a day for the past week and a half. I had never felt so completely worn down in my entire life. It was hopeless. Everything was hopeless. I couldn't stop crying, and after a while, I couldn't breathe.

Forget it. I had to tell them about the fine. I'd give them the money I'd earned so far to help pay it off, but I had to tell them. There was no getting around it.

I had to confess.

I *would* confess.

But first, I had to calm down. I still had to do all these people's work so they wouldn't get mad at me tomorrow. *Fifteen minutes, Maya,* I told myself, forcing a deep breath into my lungs. *You've got another fifteen minutes to freak out, and then you gotta pull it together for one more night.*

It ended up being thirty minutes of freaking out, but by one in the morning, I was calm. Composed. Full of resolve, if completely dehydrated from the torrent of tears. Just a few more assignments to do tonight, then confession tomorrow. The consequences would be dire, but at least I'd be able to sleep again . . . probably on the plane to Thailand, where I'd be stuck in boarding school as all my friends went off to college and had great lives and forgot all about me. But at least I wouldn't be lying anymore. I wouldn't *have* to lie anymore. I put my hair up into a no-nonsense bun, then peeked out my door; the house was dark. Time to get a Diet Coke from the kitchen and then suck it up for one more night.

I tiptoed down the stairs, congratulating myself on keeping their creaking to a minimum, although I had to hold in the urge to swear when my foot slipped off the edge of the bottom step and I was forced to grab the railing to keep from falling. I headed toward the kitchen, but then saw a sliver of light shining from the den. *Huh.* Were my parents awake? My mom usually does all her accounting stuff in there, at a big used desk my parents bought when they first came to America. On the wall over it, all of our restaurant memorabilia is hung on a big corkboard—mostly copies of the reviews we also have hung up at the restaurant itself, plus some reviews of the other Thai restaurants in town if there's something negative in them. (It makes my Dad laugh.) There are also copies of the first order slip they ever took, the first personal check, and the first credit card receipt from back when credit card machines were actually those big plastic and metal things you had to manually slide. But my mom usually works on accounting first thing in the morning, so maybe she or my dad was just having a bout of insomnia or something. Nope, not so much—as I approached the den and gently pushed open the door to peek in, I saw my mom asleep, half-slumped over the computer keyboard.

They say you look younger when you're asleep, but my mom didn't look younger. She just looked tired.

I pondered waking her up, then pondered getting a blanket for her. Not that it was at all necessary, given that the den, which is barely bigger than a closet, traps heat like crazy and is the warmest room in the house by far. At a loss for the moment, I glanced at the computer to see what she was doing. On the screen was an Excel worksheet, and there were a bunch of red numbers throughout it. Wait, was our restaurant losing money?

Neither Nat nor I knew much about our income, because my parents pretty much subscribed to the "keep the kids in the dark" theory of family finances, but I had to assume that we were doing *okay*, at least. Nobody was starving, and we had a roof over our heads. On the other hand, businesspeople everywhere didn't use the term "in the red" for nothing. Red numbers were bad.

I took a few steps closer to the screen. I knew we weren't exactly rich, and I knew that Nat and I needed all the scholarships and financial aid we could get in order to pay for college, but . . . were we broke? Were we too broke to pay the fine? Were we too broke to pay for *anything*? I squinted, trying to figure out what the hell was going on, wishing I knew better how loans or credit cards or running a business worked, then tentatively reached out a hand to hit the down arrow button.

My mom moved. I froze.

"Hi," I said softly.

"Hello," she said. "Whoops. Fell asleep." She smiled at me, rubbing her eyes and then her arms in their night-gown sleeves. She reached for the mouse to click her Excel sheet closed, then shut down the computer and yawned and stretched while the not-exactly-state-of-the-art machine went through its usual series of tired-sounding hums and buzzes before finally powering down. "Why are you still awake?" she asked, putting her arm around me and steering me toward the door.

"Homework," I said wearily, leaning the side of my head against the side of hers. It was the truth, after all.

"You work too hard," Mom said sleepily.

"So do you," I said.

We walked up the stairs together, giggling a little bit at the extra creaking that was being created by four feet rattling up the steps simultaneously, and for a split second I considered moving my planned confession to right that very moment. But then, as I thought about the string of red numbers I'd seen on the computer screen, I suddenly knew

I was *never* going to tell my parents about the fine. Not if our restaurant was going down. Not if we were broke. They had enough to worry about; they had two kids to support. I couldn't make it worse.

This was my $10,000 mess, and it was up to me to get us out of it.

chapter nine

So. Assuming a generous rate of fifteen assignments per week for the next month, I was still only going to have made about seven grand by the time I needed to pay off the fine. Plus, I was almost certain to be hallucinating from lack of sleep; that morning when the alarm went off, I could have sworn the little panda clock was advancing steadily toward me, having grown bloody fangs inside its mouth and somehow acquired an AK-47 and a grenade. As I got ready for school, I pondered calling the Health Department to see if I could get an extension or pay in installments, but I was always the worst at prank phone calls during our middle school slumber parties (leading Sarah and Cat to *always* force me to make them whenever we played Truth or Dare), and I wasn't convinced that I could make the Health Department believe I was an adult on the phone. They'd probably hear one sentence and ask if I was trying to sell

Girl Scout cookies. Yeah, that wasn't going to work. I needed to be able to do this simply—just go over there, hand them the money, make sure the restaurant's record was clean, and move on.

So I needed cash, and fast.

Looked like Camden's other friends were gonna get their wish.

Hey need 2 talk 2 u about something. Meet me after school? I texted him at lunch, as I headed toward my usual table by the window with Cat, Sarah, and Jonny. He answered almost immediately with *Sure what about?*, which meant that I had to do an abrupt about-face and go in the opposite direction in order to answer him—I didn't need my friends looking at my phone over my shoulder and seeing what I was doing. I walked back outside the cafeteria door and hovered in the hallway as I texted Camden back with *Tell u when I c u.* This time, there was no answer, so after a few minutes of standing around, trying to look casual while repeatedly looking at my phone, I headed back into the cafeteria and sat down to eat lunch.

"How come you were coming over here and suddenly you turned around?" Sarah asked as I unwrapped my sandwich. Drat, so she'd seen me.

"Uh, I forgot . . . my . . . lunch in my locker," I said lamely, eliciting a quizzical look from her as she munched her way through a carrot stick. *Ugh.* Why couldn't I have said "the bathroom" or something simple like that? My brain was apparently even more fried than I thought, so I was glad when Cat decided not to eat her Skittles, instead passing the bag across the table to me. I took a handful and gave the rest to Jonny, who pounced on them with relish. I ate mine slowly, hoping for enough of a sugar rush to get me through the rest of the day awake, if not actually alert.

That afternoon after the last bell, Camden loped up to my locker and then broke into a grin when I took his wrist and yanked him toward the student parking lot.

"Wow, I've been fantasizing about this forever," he said, purposely resisting for a second before falling into step beside me.

"Shut up," I said, dropping my hand from his arm. "This is just better discussed out of the hearing range of the entire school, that's all." In the hallway, Dave Markley passed by us, low-fiving Camden on the way while completely ignoring me.

"Still taking Double D to the Fling, dude?" he asked.

"As a friend, yeah," answered Camden.

"Friend with benefits?" Dave smirked. He was now a few feet down the hall from us and walking backward.

"Do I have any other kind?" Camden called over his shoulder after him, and they both laughed. "What?" Camden asked me, noticing that I was rolling my eyes.

"Nothing," I said. "Well, you disgust me, but other

than that, nothing," I added, shaking my head as we reached the parking lot and got into his car. Camden just laughed, then stuck the key in the ignition and started rolling down the windows. It was a warmish day finally, sunny and in the mid-forties—practically T-shirt weather for me, and apparently for Camden as well. He pulled his sweatshirt up over his head and chucked it into the backseat.

"Close the windows," I said.

"Of course. All the better to steam 'em up." He yanked down on his green-and-gray ringer, which had ridden up during the sweatshirt removal, then jokingly reached toward me. I smacked his arm away.

"See aforementioned disgust," I said, shoving the backpack on my lap slightly to the left in order to act as a barrier between us. "I just don't want anyone to hear what we're talking about." I shrugged my jacket off and put it on top of the backpack for good measure.

"Because you're gonna talk dirty?" Camden asked cheerfully. He hit the button that started rolling the windows back up.

"You have a one-track mind," I said.

"Half a track," he replied. The windows were now closed, and he twisted in his seat slightly, leaning back against the driver's side door and looking at me. "So are we just gonna sit here, or did you want me to drive somewhere?"

"Uh, drive, I guess. It's weird if we just sit here." People were already looking at us through the windows, and at least one guy had pointed, although whether it was at us or at the sight of two dance team chicks in tank tops and yoga pants inexplicably doing heel stretches by the station wagon next to us, I wasn't sure. I wondered whether I was starting any new rumors just by being seen talking with Camden. Probably.

Camden started the car, and I took a deep breath as we pulled out of the parking lot and into the street. "Okay," I said. "All your friends who want me to do their homework for them? I'll do it. Whoever you've got. All of 'em." There. It was out in the open.

"I thought you said you didn't have enough time," he said, gunning past a school bus, onto the bridge over the river where our crew team was practicing, and then hanging a right.

"I'll make time," I said.

"Because you know, you're right. You look kinda trashed lately," he went on, hanging a left. He appeared to be driving totally at random; at first it had seemed like he was heading downtown, but after the last turn, I'd lost track of where he could be going.

"Thanks," I said dryly.

"You might wanna try wearing makeup," he added.

"I'll look into it."

"Or get some Botox."

"I'll borrow your mom's. So do we have a deal, or what?" I looked at him impatiently.

Camden took another random turn. "No deal. You already said before you were too tired to do that much work." he said. "You're kind of slipping up already, frankly."

"I am not slipping up!" I said defensively.

"I got a D minus in Algebra the other day, and you're supposed to be aiming for a C minus," he pointed out. "Frankly, I should get some money back or something."

"Whatever," I said. "That's not a big deal. I'll average it out on the next assignment—"

"Forget it," Camden said, turning randomly yet again. "I'm not gonna tell my friends to pay good money for a lousy product."

"Camden, please," I said quietly. I could hear the desperation in my own voice . . . and when he pulled the car over to the side of the road, put it in park, and fixed his gaze on me steadily, I knew he'd heard it too.

"What's wrong?" he asked, his voice low.

I sighed and closed my eyes. Camden sat there silently, waiting, watching as I steeled myself for what was about to happen. Finally, I opened them—and told him. Told him everything. About my parents leaving me in charge at the restaurant, about what I'd done that weekend, about the Health Department fine. About the fact that there was no freaking way my family had the money to cover it. About the fact that if my parents found out what had happened, I would be shipped off to boarding school in Thailand for sure.

"Not that you care," I said finally, my voice breaking a little. "But . . . that's why I need to make money. I know I'm tired. I know I'm starting to slip, and I'm sorry. I'll drink more Red Bull. I'll eat nothing but coffee ice cream for the next month. But please . . . seriously. If any of your friends want in, let me do it. Okay?"

Camden sat there silently. A long moment passed.

"No," he said.

I drew my knees up to my chest and leaned my forehead toward them, not caring that I was putting my shoes on his fancy black leather seats. I made a truly valiant effort to keep from beginning to cry.

"You shouldn't do it," Camden continued. "What you *should* do is get some of your nerdy friends to help you out."

"What?" I asked, lifting my head to look at him. He wasn't actually suggesting that I—?

"Your friends," he repeated, eyeing my shoes but not saying anything about it. "You've got friends, right? That scrawny little guy? That alterna-girl? That fat chick?"

"Sarah is not fat," I snapped. She isn't. She just isn't anorexic like all *his* friends.

"Of course not, she's a healthy woman of today," he

said, not missing a beat. "Seriously, though, that's what you should do. Get your friends to do it. Pay 'em like, seventy-five bucks each, and pocket the rest. You'll pay off that fine in no time." He was sitting up straighter now, and his eyes were beginning to flash with a smidge of excitement.

"I can't do that!" I exclaimed. "I can't do that to my friends. That's disgusting!"

"Okay, then don't." Camden shrugged. "Have fun in Thailand. Although I doubt your parents would actually ship you off, by the way."

"Yeah, well, we don't all have nice parents who let us do whatever the hell we want," I snapped.

"My parents aren't nice, they just aren't ever around," he retorted. "That's the only reason I can do whatever I want."

"That and all the money they throw at you," I said.

"Maybe my dad's just a better businessman than your dad," he snapped. My jaw dropped open, and for a split second Camden actually looked sorry. We sat in silence for a minute, each of us realizing that we'd totally gotten to the other one.

"Well," I said finally, too tired to start a shouting match. "Your idea is technically a good one, but it's evil. I can't be that evil."

"Sure you can. You need to pay off that fine, don't you?"

He had a point.

"I mean, what are you gonna do," he added, "just let your family's restaurant go down in flames?"

He had a very, very good point. I stared out the window with a sigh, clutching my knees to my chin. I closed my eyes and forced myself to breathe as the past several days of depression and exhaustion condensed in my stomach, then twisted, then slowly turned into a tiny knot of resolve.

I turned back to Camden. "Let me talk to my friends."

Camden smiled. "Good girl." He reached out and punched me ever so lightly on the shoulder, then looked around. "Where the hell are we, anyway?"

"I don't know. You were the one driving," I said. I couldn't tell where we were either; outside the window it just looked like a bunch of trees with no houses in sight. No street signs, either.

"I was driving randomly," he said. "*Huh.* I have no idea what just happened." He started up the car again and pulled into the road, then decided to make a U-turn. Another car came barreling toward us from over a hill, and Camden started to try and get quickly in front of it. He probably could've made it, but at the last second he thought better of it and backed up a little instead.

"Sissy," I said.

Camden didn't respond, but when I glanced over, I saw he was smiling.

✦

Half an hour later, after Camden had finally figured out that he'd somehow driven us onto the service road of the University Botanical Gardens, I set foot in the tutoring office for the first time in almost two weeks. Jonny was in a room with Hilary, Cat was in a room with a giant football player whose name I didn't know, one of the other rooms was occupied by some sophomore Physical Science study group, and Sarah was in the main room with Leonard, working on what appeared to be a Biology outline; they probably had a couple students who were in the same class. As I walked in, they both looked up at me, surprised.

"Maya! Long time no convo! You look hot," Leonard said.

"Yeah, uh . . . what's up," I said, giving Sarah a wave and dropping my backpack on the floor.

"I finished that new song," Leonard said, fidgeting with the twine necklace he was wearing, which looked jarringly out of place against his button-down shirt. "Wanna hear it? I don't have my guitar here, but I could probably do it a cappella."

"Uh . . . I'll wait for the guitar," I said, taking a seat at the table.

"You sure?" asked Leonard.

"One hundred percent certain," I said, exchanging an amused glance with Sarah.

"Hey there," she said. "What are you doing here? Did Camden suddenly—"

"Camden King? Hey, did you really hook up with him?" Leonard interrupted. "Because I heard he got like, six girls pregnant last year. So you might want to get yourself tested, or start double-bagging it, or both—"

"I didn't hook up with him," I snapped, scooching back in my chair. "Whatever you heard, you heard wrong. I'm just killing some time until I gotta go to work, and I didn't feel like doing it in the library, okay?" *Ugh*, why was Leonard even there? If he didn't leave soon, I was going to have to get Jonny, Cat, and Sarah to follow me somewhere else, which would look totally suspicious. I picked up my backpack off the floor and threw it onto the couch, then followed it, pulling out my French textbook to get started on next week's composition. (I'd taken to doing my own homework in any pocket of free time I had, even if it meant jumping ahead to stuff that wasn't even due yet.) Then I waited for the longest forty-eight minutes of my life, aside from that day freshman year when I forgot to put on my regular bra after taking off my sports bra at the end of Gym class. Not as big a deal for me—literally—as it would've been for, say, Stacey Ray, but it was still majorly uncomfortable as I waited for the bell to ring so I could rush back to the locker room. Finally the

Physical Science study group and Leonard all finished up what they were doing and left, Leonard waving energetically at me on his way out, and I mustered enough energy to give a halfhearted half wave back.

Okay. There was nobody in the tutoring office except for me and my friends; Mrs. Hunter had taken off early, and Jonny's and Cat's respective students were on their way out the door too.

"What now, ladies?" asked Jonny. He and Cat came out of their study rooms and plunked themselves into seats at the big table where Sarah was sitting; I got up off the couch and moved over there too. "Maya's gotta work in a few, but does anybody wanna do something?" He used his shirtsleeve to polish his glasses as he talked. "Mall? Pleasant stroll downtown? Unpleasant stroll uptown?"

"Do we even have an uptown?" asked Cat.

"Unpleasant stroll downtown?" Jonny amended. Sarah and Cat both gave him a bemused look, and Cat playfully reached out to muss his blond spikes.

"Hey, guys," I interrupted. Loudly.

They all looked at me and I took a deep breath. "All right, I'm not really tutoring Camden King."

"Big surprise there," Cat and Jonny said at the same time. They turned to look at each other and grinned. Sarah didn't say anything, but she'd gone a little pale and her eyes were very nearly taking up the entire top half of her face. I tried to avoid her gaze as she nervously scrunched her hands into the sleeves of her pale blue sweater and then rested her chin on them. She stared at me, silently waiting.

"He's actually been paying me to do his homework for him," I continued. Underneath the table, my feet were tapping nervously.

"Shut. Up!" Cat leaned to the side to give me a full-body shove. "How much do you charge?"

Everything that had happened in the last week flashed before my eyes: the restaurant, the fine, Camden's homework, everyone else's homework, the money, the red numbers on my mom's computer, Camden pointing out that I could take money off the top from my friends if I wanted. . . .

"It depends on the assignment," I lied. "Usually seventy-five."

If I'd been going to hell before, now I was going to superhell.

"Shut up!" Cat said again, sounding thoroughly delighted. "You vixen! You cheating little whore! You immoral, vile, foul fiend . . . ess! Fiendette! Fienderina!" She took off one of the six silver rings she was wearing on various fingers and gleefully plunked it on the tabletop.

"That's cheating," Sarah said flatly. Inside her sleeves, I could see her hands beginning to curl into fists.

"It's profitable cheating," Jonny pointed out. "Seriously,

dude," he said, turning to me with a look of grudging admiration. "That's kind of a lot of money. I mean, even if you did just like, two extra homework assignments a day for a week . . ." His fingers started inching toward his calculator, then stopped—it wasn't like he couldn't do the math in his head.

"I know," I said. Jonny's and Cat's relaxed, even positive attitudes were making me feel much better about the entire thing, although the fact that Sarah's eyes were shooting daggers at all of us was dampening my mood slightly. "So the question is, do you guys want in?" I looked at the three of them, hoping against hope.

The door opened and Leonard bounced back into the room. "Into what?" he asked.

"Into bowling this weekend," I said quickly. Christ, had he heard anything? I moved one hand under the table and crossed my fingers that he hadn't.

"You guys bowl?" he asked.

"We do. Big time," I answered. Jonny and Cat both vigorously nodded their heads. Sarah just sat there.

"Cool, well, maybe I'll take it up and we can all go together sometime. Or just, you know, you and me, Maya." He grabbed a pencil case off the table—"Forgot this"—and took off again.

The door clicked shut. We waited. He didn't come back.

"Hey, Maya," Cat said, nudging me with an amused glance. "Put your head between your knees. Your face is like, totally white right now."

"God, that was close," I said, shaking off my panic. Yikes, if he'd heard . . . "Anyway," I continued, "Camden's friends are totally in on it now too, and they've got just as much money as he does, and it's really easy to do, because it's not like you have to do a good job, so . . . what do you guys think?"

"How long have you been at it?" asked Jonny.

"I don't know, not that long," I said. "We haven't been caught yet, but yeah . . . not that long."

Jonny and Cat looked at each other, and Cat shrugged. "All right, hook us up," said Cat. "Why the hell not?"

"Yeah . . . I guess," Jonny said hesitantly, then realized something. "Oh, dude, I could pay my insurance off so much faster. . . ." He'd rear-ended someone the very first time his parents had let him drive alone, and they'd immediately told him that the raised rate was his problem. "Yeah," he said, more definite-sounding now. "Yeah, okay."

"Sweet," I said. We all looked over at Sarah, who shook her head emphatically. Then she glared at me.

"Well, I'll talk to Camden tonight and figure stuff out and let you guys know tomorrow what the deal is," I said, guiltily avoiding Sarah's eyes.

"Cool," Jonny said. He and Cat grabbed their books and backpacks and got up. Sarah didn't.

"You coming, Sare?" Cat asked, pausing with her hand on the door handle.

"In a minute," Sarah answered quietly. She waited for them to leave, then shut the door, sat back down, and turned to me.

"What the *hell* do you think you're doing?" she shouted at the top of her lungs.

"Oh my God, you never yell—" I started.

"I do when you're being like this! You're gonna get caught, and you're gonna get expelled! And even if you don't, it's still wrong!"

"Sarah, calm down—"

"I will *not* calm down!" Her face was beginning to turn red. "I just witnessed my three best friends going completely nuts on me!"

"Sarah!"

"I'm totally turning you in. I'm turning you in. I'm turning you in right now—"

I grabbed her arm, even though she hadn't actually moved anywhere. "Sarah. You can't turn us in."

"Fine," she said, yanking her arm away while violently scooting her chair a foot back. "I'm not turning you in. But I can't believe you're doing this. What do you need the money for? You work at the restaurant. You get tips all the time."

"Come on, you know how it works. When's the last time my mom let us keep any of that?" I asked. "It's for college." *And according to my mom's computer, there doesn't seem to be that much of it,* I mentally added.

"So?" Sarah asked.

"So," I said, trying to think of why I would be doing something so illegal if I didn't have that stupid fine to pay off. "So maybe you don't realize this, but it's sort of a pain to work my ass off every single day of my life and not be allowed to buy *anything* nice or *anything* cool for myself with any of the money that *I'm* earning! Okay? So maybe I'm moonlighting!" I stood up, getting into it now, and started pacing back and forth. "Maybe for once I wanna go to the mall and buy something cute and not have to ask my parents for the money, even though I just worked a five-hour shift making *them* money! Okay? God! If you don't want in, you don't have to be in, but you also don't have to get all judgmental on me about it!" Wow. I had been making all that stuff up to try and convince Sarah that I was pissed off enough about my life to do something this shady, but now that I heard what I was saying, I was even convincing myself.

Apparently not her, though. Without saying anything, she got up, grabbed her stuff, and left the tutoring office, and instead of carefully closing the door behind her as usual, she left it wide open—Sarah's version of a slam.

I stood there, stricken for a moment. Sarah and I had fought probably twice in our whole lives, and I'd never seen her even *nearly* this angry. I pondered running after her and spilling the entire story about the fine, but I knew that she wouldn't think it justified the cheating, and I also knew she'd probably give me at least a smidge of "Well, it *was* your fault." Nope, I couldn't tell her, especially not now. But . . . did I just lose my best friend? Was she never going to speak to me again? Cat and Jonny were in on this now too . . . she couldn't just not talk to *any* of us, could she?

Should I even be worrying about this right now, given all the other stuff I had to worry about?

I didn't know.

I sighed, put my books into my backpack, and trudged to the bus stop to go to work. That night I texted Camden that I had two more people to do homework assignments; he texted back almost right away, saying that he had plenty more people who wanted in. I did another few calculations, and it looked like, if I kept on doing the homework and also took money off the top of everything Jonny and Cat did, I would just barely make my goal in time.

Well. Here went nothing.

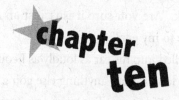

chapter
ten

"First of all," I whispered to Camden the next morning at his locker, "if you've really got like, twenty people who want in, we have to start organizing this better." Across the hall, a couple of sophomore girls were decorating some guy's locker with a long vertical pink-and-red WILL U GO 2 SPRING FLING WITH ME? banner. Ah, life imitating *Laguna Beach*. Although it wasn't that surprising—prom at our school is only for seniors, so even though the Fling was still a month away, it was a much bigger event, given that there were an extra three grades' worth of kids who got to flip out about it. I watched as the owner of the locker showed up, looking half-happy and half-terrified at the flurry of activity and the accompanying chorus of shrieks. He gave the girl who'd asked him a cutely embarrassed hug.

"Why are you whispering?" Camden whispered back at me.

"Because I'm paranoid," I whispered back.

"Nobody can hear you over those screaming chicks," he whispered back. "Are you sure it isn't just an excuse to lean in really close to my ear?"

"YEAH!" I yelled into his ear as loudly as I could, which was actually much louder than anything else going on in the hallway. Everyone within twenty feet turned to stare at us, but it was totally worth it to see Camden jerk away and fall back against the edge of his open locker. He glared at me and rubbed his shoulder. "Jesus CHRIST! What's wrong with you?"

"It amuses me to see you in pain," I said. "Although I don't really think of that as wrong." I leaned back against the row of lockers and smirked at him the way he smirked at me ninety percent of the time, which was enjoyable and got even more so when I realized he had noticed exactly what I was doing and was annoyed by it.

Camden sighed and lowered his voice as the rest of the hallway went back to activities much more fascinating than listening to us. "You know," he said, "I actually agree with you. We should talk about this somewhere else. After school? My car?"

"Sure," I answered. "You've got me for half an hour before I gotta go to work."

"You're a smart girl. You'll get the plan a lot faster than that." Camden closed his locker door and slung his messenger bag over his shoulder.

"Wait, there's a plan?" I asked.

"There's been one." He shrugged, running a hand through his hair and then starting off down the hallway.

"And you're only telling me this now?" I asked.

"No, I'm telling you after school." He swaggered away, low-fiving Derek as he passed him and sending a random group of freshman girls into a fit of giggles with a flirty grin.

I stared after him for a bit and then started trudging to class. Fine, I could wait. Mostly what I'd wanted to tell him was that I'd given Jonny and Cat the lower price, just like we'd agreed, and that he shouldn't say anything about it if he ran into them, but I figured the odds of Camden seeing either of them around and then actually speaking to them were about zero. Of course, if he did run into them and said something sketchy, I would lose all my friends. Sarah was already mad at me, but if Jonny and Cat knew I was about to totally rip them off . . .

My paranoid, self-doubting train of thought was derailed for a moment as I ducked under a giant pile of wooden sticks being carried by two crew team guys. Ah, so they were reinstating the bonfire for this year's Fling. I wondered if Cat was going to have a problem with that, being as how two years ago the thing had burned out of control and almost caught her scarf on fire. Speaking of Cat, if she and Jonny found out that I was about to exploit them for profit . . . Camden knew why I was doing it, and it seemed like he wouldn't tell, but what if something slipped out? They'd hate me forever. I'd lose all my friends. . . .

No, I told myself. *You're doing it again.* I couldn't think of it that way. Justifiable homicide, dammit. Casualties of war. I could hurt my friends a little to help my family a lot . . . just as long as they never found out.

"All right," Camden said as soon as I got in his car after school. "Here's how it's gonna work." He already had his seat belt on, and he looked all business.

"What, no 'how was your day'? You've changed," I deadpanned, letting my backpack drop down by my feet. "I feel like we're not connecting anymore."

He rolled his eyes and summoned up a fakely jovial tone of voice. "How was your day, honey?" he asked.

"Great!" I said cheerfully. "My belly ring got caught on my outfit this morning, so I had to cut off the bottom two inches of my shirt, but that's okay, because I accidentally put on too much glitter lotion anyway and somebody might as well see it. It's flavored! Want to taste my rib cage?"

He sat there, looking at me with exactly zero expression on his face.

"That was my impression of Stacey," I said.

"It was actually pretty accurate," he admitted with a small smile. "Although you forgot to adjust your boobs."

He waited. I didn't move.

"Worth a shot." He shrugged, then turned away from me and started the car. "We're gonna do laps around the block," he explained, knowing as well as I did that, now more than ever, we needed to avoid starting more rumors. "Or, I dunno, maybe I'll just drive randomly again." I nodded as we headed out of the parking lot. He deliberately slowed down as we went past the football field where the cheerleaders were practicing—not surprising at all, since today's weather was warm enough that they could ditch wearing leg warmers under their little skirts—but then sped up again as we drove off school property.

"Okay," he continued, aggressively switching lanes. "So, here's the thing. We're the ones running this operation, right? You and me. Nobody else."

"Right," I said. I winced as he got close to sideswiping another car, but nothing happened.

"So we should be the only ones who ever really know what's going on," he continued, slowing down and beginning to make a random series of lazy turns. "You know? I'll get assignments from clients, I'll give 'em to you, you and your nerdy friends will do 'em, then you'll give 'em back to me. Money changes hands only between us. You take your cut, I'll take my cut—"

"Wait, you're taking a cut too?" I asked. He hardly needed the extra money.

"Finder's fee," he said smoothly. "Not from my friends. Their price will stay the same, but any new clients? A hundred and twenty-five per assignment, at least. We can mess with the numbers, whatever, use a sliding scale. Don't worry about it—I'll handle that side."

I stared at him, mouth agape. He'd really thought this through.

Camden noticed my shock, grinned at me, and continued. "No contact between our friends, in case they decide to start independent contracting. We don't want anyone going around us. Plus, the fewer people who know what's really going on, the smaller the chances are that we'll get caught. I'm not that worried, but risk minimization is probably a good idea at this point." Camden took a right, and suddenly we were back on the University Botanical Gardens service road. At least this time, we both knew it.

"Risk mini—wow," I said. "You've thought about this a *lot*." I couldn't help it; I crossed my arms and leaned back against the passenger-side door, staring at him in grudging admiration.

"Please, I've been thinking about taking this operation big-time ever since we started—it's just that you were too tired." Camden honked at a pickup truck in front of us, which was taking way too long at a stop sign. "But now, since you're cool with expanding . . . you know, given your little situation . . ." He glanced over at me, then returned his eyes to the road.

"You were thinking about expanding since we started? What for? You don't need the money," I pointed out.

"Mostly to torture myself by hanging out with a chick who's a bitch ninety-five percent of the time." He threw me a playful glance.

I raised an eyebrow. "What am I the other five percent of the time?"

"A crazy bitch?"

"Right you are," I said. "Seriously, though, what are you doing this for?"

"What are you?" he threw back.

"You know perfectly well," I said. "To avoid getting killed by my parents long enough so that I can get into Stanford and get the hell out of this town."

"Why, they have a really cool campus or something?"

"What?" I asked, momentarily taken aback.

"Stanford. What's so great about it?"

Huh? "It's . . . it's Stanford!" I exclaimed. "It's in California, so it's far away from here, and I've seen all the pictures on their Web site, and it all looks awesome, and—"

"Wait, you haven't visited in person? How do you even know if you'd like it there?" Camden asked. He looked genuinely curious.

"We couldn't afford to go college-visiting," I said flatly, somewhat annoyed that he kind of had a point. "And I don't see how you've managed to turn this around from me asking why *you* wanted to get us into this whole cheating mess."

"Hey, I found a useful service, I wanna share it with my friends," he said lightly. "I just don't wanna share it for free." He had turned the car around and was now driving us back to school.

"Yeah, about that . . ." I started. There was a tiny bit of nervousness hopping around in my stomach.

"About what?" he asked.

"I just don't . . ." I sighed. "We have to make *absolutely* sure that my friends don't find out we're taking a cut, okay?"

"Calm down. We'll make sure," said Camden. "Anyway, even if they do find out, it's not like it's actually unfair. Think about how much work we're gonna be doing, organizing all this stuff. We gotta get paid for that somehow."

Well, he had a point there. A shady point, but a point nonetheless. I sighed again, shaking my head this time. "You're right."

"Don't I know it." Camden grinned as he pulled back into the now nearly-empty school parking lot. "Well, looks like we really are in business." He parked the car across two spaces and held his right hand out to me. I was about to shake it when somebody tapped on the window behind my head. I jumped a mile. "Aaah!"

Camden laughed. "You sound like my ex during *The Grudge*," he said, looking past me out the passenger side window. "Who's that?"

I looked to see. Then sighed. Then rolled down the window.

"Hi, Maya," said Leonard. "Hey, Camden, what up?" He waved at both of us, even though he was only like, three inches away.

"Hi," I said. Camden ignored him.

"Whatcha doing?" Leonard asked. He stepped closer to me and I instinctively leaned back toward Camden.

"Nothing you need to worry about," I said, struggling to sound polite.

"You guys going out?" Leonard peered into the car, enviously checking out the fancy, gadget-covered interior.

"She wishes," Camden said from behind me. I rolled my eyes.

"Leonard," I said patiently, "did you want something?"

"Are you still tutoring him?" Leonard asked, looking past me at Camden.

"Yeah," I said.

"Sort of," Camden said at the same time. I resisted the urge to turn around and glare at him—while I was sure, from a practical standpoint, that Leonard couldn't have heard what we were talking about, given that the entire conversation had been over by the time he tapped on the window, I was paranoid enough to think that it was still somehow possible.

"We're actually going to the tutoring office right now," I said, covering. "Wanna come?" *Ugh*, why did I say that?

"Nah, it's my day off," Leonard said. "Wanna hang out when you're done tutoring? Get coffee? Or a beer?" He chuckled at his own half joke.

Behind me, Camden snickered. "As if," he said.

Leonard looked slightly hurt but didn't answer him. "Maya? Want to?" he asked again, bouncing up and down on his toes and fiddling with his backpack straps.

"Yeah, she really wants to hang with the Asian Harry Potter," Camden said, giving Leonard a disdainful head-to-toe glance. I reached back and elbowed him in the ribs, then turned to Leonard, who was now self-consciously toying with his glasses.

"Sorry, I can't," I said. I tried to sound apologetic but was pretty sure I didn't.

"Maybe tomorrow?" Leonard asked hopefully. Camden muffled a laugh, earning him another elbow to the ribs from me, as I tried to say in as gentle a tone as possible, "Probably not, but thanks."

"Okay," Leonard said quietly, looking wounded. "See

ya." He wandered away, pausing to throw another hurt look back at us before turning around and leaving for real.

"That kid wants to bone you," said Camden.

I elbowed him yet again. "Do you think he heard anything?" I asked, feeling slightly guilty at not having been particularly nice to Leonard, but mostly worried about our little scheme possibly being discovered.

"Other than his own perverted thoughts about boning you? No," Camden said. "Calm down. You panic way too easily."

"You're the one who's using terms like 'risk minimization'!" I exclaimed. "This school is such a rumor mill. Do you realize the amount of people who will be gossiping about us if I'm seen in your car too much?" I glanced out his window, saw a few stragglers coming out of the school doors, and pondered ducking below the level of the window for a moment before deciding against it.

"Well, if you're even scared of working from my car, where do you want to talk about this stuff when we really get it going?" Camden asked.

"Do we have to talk at all?" I countered.

"What do you mean?"

"Okay, I mean, obviously we have to every once in a while," I said. "But for pretty straightforward stuff, can't you just like, when you get assignments from whoever, just put 'em in my locker at some point during the day, and I can put them back in yours once they're done?"

Camden studied me. "That involves us giving each other our locker combinations," he pointed out.

"Yeah, I know," I said.

"Are we ready for that much intimacy?" he asked innocently.

I rolled my eyes as I disentangled myself from the seat belt and got out of his car. "We're hormone-addled teenagers. Aren't we supposed to do it even if we're not ready?"

The grin on his face told me he agreed.

There were a few assignments and xeroxed book pages in my locker the next day after school, with a Post-it from Camden explaining due dates and what grade or credit level needed to be achieved. He also put which assignments were for whom, although that was just for my own information; it certainly wasn't anything I was going to pass down to Cat and Jonny, in the interest of keeping everyone besides me and Camden in the dark as much as possible. I finished packing my backpack, which was already heavy with one of Camden's textbooks that he'd forgotten to xerox the pages for, and then headed to the tutoring office, where I found my friends. I dragged them into one of the study rooms and shut the door.

"All right, guys," I said, trying to sound businesslike as I rifled through the relevant papers and books. "Here are your assignments. Cat, you're doing some math for tonight and some Chem for Monday. Jonny, you're writing an English paper, which is due tomorrow."

"What's it on?" he asked.

"*Leaves of Grass.*"

"Leaves of Ass," he said instantly.

"Hilarious," I said.

"Ain't it?" Jonny smirked and high-fived his own right hand with his left one. I tossed Derek's copy of *Leaves of Grass* at him and he thumbed through it. "Are you aware that the owner of this has drawn a flipbook across most of the pages?" He peered at the pages through his glasses, then slid them down so he could flip through it over their top edge.

"No," I said. I took the book from him. There was a flipbook drawn in the corner of a pair of boobs that grew and grew until they finally burst in a shower of confetti.

"That's not bad," Cat said, reaching over my shoulder to flip the flipbook again.

"Yeah, I kinda gotta give the guy credit," I agreed, handing the book back to Jonny. Wait, I'd just revealed that this particular customer was male. Well, whatever, no big deal there. The security didn't have to be one hundred percent anonymous on all levels; it just had to be mostly that way.

"Anyway," I continued, "Jonny, it's all you. It's five pages, and it doesn't have to be any good."

"Sweet," he said.

"Your stuff can suck too, Cat," I said.

"Awesome." She grinned.

"Seriously, it if takes either of you any more than like, an hour, tops, you're trying way too hard." I leaned back in my chair and stretched, glad that everything was going smoothly so far.

"Oh, this won't take me an hour," Cat said, looking at the xeroxed pages of Stacey's math book and smiling to herself. "Unless I get distracted looking at Stacey's doodling," She showed me the papers—in between most of the math problems were loopy, flowery versions, in various handwritten fonts, of "Stacey Ray-Depp," "Stacey Ray-Bloom," and "Stacey Ray-Timberlake." Oh, great. So much for security there. Well, as long as Cat and Stacey never spoke to each other, which they never would, everything would be fine. Right?

Cat flipped through the rest of Stacey's pages with a bemused look on her face, then showed me a heart-covered "Stacey Ray–My Chemical Romance."

"Either she's really dumb, or she's kinda funny," said Cat.

We thought about that for a moment.

"She's really dumb," we said at the same time.

The next day, after Camden paid me for the homework, I handed Jonny and Cat seventy-five bucks each, along with their new assignments.

"Thanks," Jonny said, flipping through his stack of bills with relish. "It's so cool that you managed to turn tutoring the biggest dipwad in school into something profitable."

"Oh, lemons, lemonade, you know," I said, smiling as I watched him.

"I mean, you should get paid for even having to talk to Camden," Cat added, taking the new xeroxed assignment pages I had pulled out of my backpack. I felt all the blood drain from my face as I realized the implication of what she was saying, and I prayed that neither of them noticed. Christ, I was a horrible person, wasn't I? I should be shot. Hanged. Drawn and quartered. Cheating the school system was fine; I mean, it wasn't, but whatever, I was over that. Cheating my friends—I was having a bigger problem with that. *No*, I told myself. I couldn't think of it that way. Camden and I *did* deserve some extra cash for masterminding and running this operation. Plus, I was only doing it to save my parents' business, and it wasn't like Jonny and Cat weren't making a *ton* more money than they would have from tutoring. Sure, I felt guilty, but they were *psyched* to pocket that much cash for so little work, and indeed, my guilt dissolved as they both stuffed their new piles of twenties in their wallets with satisfaction and gleefully looked at each other.

"Mall?" asked Cat, theatrically pulling some oversize shades out of her purse; it was a sunny day.

"Mall," answered Jonny with a grin. "No reason not to spend this all in one place." He turned to me. "Wanna come, Maya?"

"I have to work," I said.

"I know, but it'd be wrong if we didn't at least invite you." He and Cat cheerfully took off as I reached into my pocket and clutched the money that I'd made off of the work that they'd done. Nope. They weren't doing anything wrong. The person doing that, even though it was for a good cause, was me.

chapter
eleven

Once we had everything in place, it was kind of easy to fall into our new cheating ring schedule. Camden and I would ignore each other at school—no point feeding the rumors and thereby attracting attention—but after sixth period every day, I'd find a sheaf of papers in my locker: assignment sheets and xeroxed copies of the necessary book pages from Camden and his friends, covered in multi-colored Post-it notes detailing what needed to be done. This meant that Camden was either eating the cost of xeroxing, or he'd managed to figure out the code to the machines in the library. I was assuming it was the latter, because otherwise the copying would've really been adding up, and there was no way he wouldn't be figuring it into the "operation costs" or some other fancy business term. I'd distribute the assignments to Cat and Jonny before heading off to work, get them the next morning, and then stick everything back in Camden's locker before school started. He'd distribute them back to his pals, and then it was just up to each of his friends to make sure they copied the assignments over in their own handwriting before handing them in.

Which, of course, was my first mistake. A few days in, Derek got lazy and totally didn't bother to copy his over; he just handed in the exact problem set that Jonny had done for him, in Jonny's handwriting. Nothing of note happened to him, and Camden purposely told me about it in order to try and stem my constant jitters that we were always just millimeters away from getting caught, but after that I got even more paranoid and came up with a preventative measure—I started drawing obscene highlighter doodles all over the pages that I gave to Camden, so that there was no way his friends could just hand in the same stuff we gave them without copying it over first.

"Here," I said, the morning after the lazy, stupid Derek incident, as I intercepted Camden on his way to his locker shortly before the first-period bell and dragged him into an empty physics lab. I handed him three problem sets with the words *PECKER* and *BALLS* written all over them in multicolored highlighters, plus pictures of stick-figure people having sex in different positions. "This is to force your douche-bag friends to copy over the stuff in their own handwriting before they hand it in. There's no way I'm letting us get caught just because our clients get lazy." I crossed my arms and stared at him, daring him to get mad.

He didn't. He just looked at the papers, surprised, then looked at me. "That's actually a really good idea," he said, sounding impressed.

"I know," I said.

"And these pictures you drew are weirdly hot."

"I don't disagree," I said. "By the way, I'm charging you for the highlighters I bought."

I think he might've said "I love you" as I walked out of the classroom, but the hallway was noisy, so I couldn't be sure.

At least it was easier for typed papers; I just printed them and handed them off, no highlighting necessary. I was already in the habit of throwing in spelling mistakes that the spellchecker wouldn't catch, like the wrong version of *affect/effect*, but after a while, Cat and Jonny took to amusing themselves by getting even more creatively shameless. One time, Jonny handed in the reading comprehension questions for Tim O'Brien's *Tha Thingz They Carried*, and Cat e-mailed me a file for Brad's *Red Badge of Courage* paper with the title "Terror In The Soldier."

"Not subtle," I told her.

"Dumb kids aren't." She shrugged.

"That's not even a good title," I added.

"That's the beauty—it doesn't have to be."

This was true.

Word started getting around, and our client list grew. Some customers actually started wanting a *good* job done on their assignments, which we charged more for, but which took a lot longer, of course. Once, somebody even wanted an A, which meant that I basically had to do my three-page history paper twice, trying just as hard both times. At least it was to the tune of nearly two hundred bucks. And while Jonny and Cat were eager to do more once they realized, after a few days, just how easy it all was, I couldn't really manage it all, because I was still holding down a waitressing shift every night, and Camden's pals' demand was starting to outweigh our supply.

"Can't you get some of your other friends in on it?" Camden asked about a week in, after I explained to him that some of our clients were just going to have to do their own work some of the time, because Jonny, Cat, and I couldn't handle the workload. We were in his car, doing our usual thing of using it as an office where we could discuss business, only now we'd added the extra precautionary measure of him picking me up about a block away from school and randomly driving around town, so that nobody would see us leave together. "Wait," he stopped himself, simultaneously braking for a red light. "Do you *have* any other friends? Oh my God, you only have like, three friends, don't you?"

"Only three that I trust with this stuff and only two

who are willing to do it," I said matter-of-factly. Sarah had reached an uneasy truce with the three of us—that is, after the first big blowup, she'd just opted to pretend that nothing had happened—but I occasionally noticed her narrowing her eyes whenever she saw us exchanging assignment papers or cash, and she absolutely *glared* at Camden whenever we happened to pass by him in the hallway, although he never noticed. She didn't say anything to anybody about the cheating ring, and I knew she wouldn't, but along with her "Don't tell" was a whole lot of "Don't ask."

"Are you sure?" Camden raised his eyebrows at me. "Have you asked around?"

"It's just—no, I haven't, actually," I said.

"Well, why not?"

"Because . . ." I trailed off. I didn't really have an excuse, actually. As far as I knew, we weren't even remotely close to getting caught, and everything was running like clockwork. If this were any other business, it would *absolutely* be time to expand. And I could certainly use the extra money—the way things were going, I might almost make it to my goal in time, but I'd probably have to supplement the money by skimming tips at work without my mom seeing. I'd been doing it anyway lately, just as an extra precaution, but in tiny quantities so that she wouldn't suspect. (At least, I assumed she wasn't suspecting—sometimes it seemed like she had eyes not just in the back of her own head, but in everyone else's as well.) As I got closer to the fine's due date, depending on our clients' workloads, I was definitely going to have to ramp the tip-skimming up. Unless . . . well, unless we expanded the cheating ring instead.

"Let me think about it," I said. "I'm not sure who else I can ask." Maybe Cat's little sister? Maybe Jonny's? Maybe some of the other tutors? Maaaybe Sarah again?

I pictured the look on her face the day she'd blown up at me. Okay, not Sarah.

"You'll think of someone," Camden said, reaching over to fiddle with the radio station; there wasn't anything on his presets that wasn't a commercial, so he punched the power button off. "Hey, maybe if you get enough people, you could retire, you know? Live off of the commissions. Like a real estate agent. Or a pimp." He grinned at me.

"Doubt it. I need all the money I can get," I said flatly.

"Well then, remember you can get more money if you get more people," Camden said.

Damn him for always having good points. He could probably convince me to become a meth addict, if he were given enough time to think up some smooth arguments.

"I'll ask around, okay?" I said, sighing. "I'll see what we can do."

"Okay. By the way, Stacey and Dani wanna take you shopping, so I gave 'em your number."

What?

After school that day, I hit up the tutoring office and pulled Jonny and Cat into one of the study rooms as usual. Sarah was the only other person in the office; her student hadn't gotten there yet, so she was on the couch, busily working her way through her copy of *The Aeneid*, the pages already covered with a ton of those little colored tape tabs she liked to use. I thought about how fast she could write an English paper, and I started to hope against hope that I could possibly be as persuasive as Camden and make her change her mind.

"Sarah, do you wanna maybe come in?" I asked tentatively, pausing in the doorway, my hand on the doorknob.

"What're you talking about in there?" she asked, looking up and brushing her hair back from her face.

I didn't say anything—I knew that she knew.

"Okay, then no," she said, looking back down at her book again.

"Sorry, I just thought that maybe . . ." I trailed off.

"Nope," she said, into the pages instead of to me.

"Okay, thanks anyway," I said, inching into the study room and closing the door. I turned to Cat and Jonny, leaned back against the door, and sighed.

"She's never gonna do it," said Cat.

"I know," I said.

"But she's never gonna tell, either," added Jonny.

"I know that too. We all know that." Bless her freakin' heart.

Cat and Jonny settled into chairs, Cat opening up a bag of Goldfish crackers and offering it to the both of us. I perched on the edge of the table and threw the idea of getting more people in on the action at them.

"So . . . I dunno," I said. "What do you think? Hell, *who* do you think? Anyone?" I crunched on a goldfish; it helped me to seem casual instead of nervous.

"What about Nat?" suggested Jonny.

Oh, no way. Too close to home, literally. "No," I said flatly. "I'm not involving him, and you guys better not tell him, either," I added.

"Okay, but—"

"But nothing," I said, cutting Jonny off. "He's my little brother, and if this thing goes down in flames—which it won't, but if it does—I'm not dragging him down with me." That was the truth, actually, but mostly it was because if Nat heard that I was suddenly trying to make scads of money illegally, it would probably take him all of three seconds to put two and two together and figure out what had happened at the restaurant. No, it was better that he stayed in the dark about everything. "Besides, he'd probably react like

Sarah and tell my parents. I'm not having it, so, end of discussion," I added.

I knew Jonny and Cat were looking at each other and wondering why I was so paranoid—I could feel it in both their raised eyebrows. "What about your sisters?" I asked them both quickly.

"Dude, my sister's a freshman," said Jonny.

"So? Half our clients have the brains of freshmen. Some of 'em *are* freshmen."

"Really?" he asked.

"They will be if we get more people to do this work," I said. "Trust me. Clients aren't the problem. Camden knows everyone." I twirled a pencil nervously in my fingers.

"My sister would totally do it," Cat said, eyeing the pencil I was twirling and then trying to do it herself with a pen. It flipped out of her fingers almost immediately and fell to the floor. She made a face at it.

"Sweet," I said, putting my pencil down. Bella, Cat's sister, is cool. She's a year younger than us and could practically be Cat's clone . . . if Cat were five feet ten inches tall and a volleyball player.

"I guess I can ask Jill," said Jonny. "Although, if *you're* scared about Nat getting in trouble—"

"Awesome," I said, stopping him before he started getting too worried. "It'll be fine. It's just that, I mean, Nat's way too busy with Science Olympiad and all that stuff to be able to do it anyway. Can you guys think of anyone else?" I picked the pencil up again, grabbed a legal pad, and we started making a list. The people we could trust, and who had the ability, and who would likely be willing, comprised a small overlap indeed—if I'd drawn a Venn diagram, the middle part would have barely been a pinpoint.

But two days later, there were seven of us smart kids doing more than thirty rich kids' homework assignments.

The day after that, I fell asleep in all six of my classes.

The day after *that*, I did a quick calculation and realized that I could make enough money to pay the fine off by commissions alone. Barely, but I could do it.

And the day after that, I told Camden I wanted to retire.

"That. Is. Awesome," he said. We were in his car, he was speeding as usual, and he kept one hand on the steering wheel while holding up the other for a high five. "You're gonna rock it like me? Pimp-daddy style?"

"Indeed," I said, tapping my palm to his. "If that's how you insist on putting it." Seriously though, retirement sounded good. Wait, no. It sounded *great*.

"Sweet. Then we have time to hang now," he said.

"What?" I glanced at him sideways, somewhat taken aback.

"You've been all zonked because you've been working too hard, but now you won't be anymore," Camden said, as if the idea of spending time together outside our little business was the most natural thing in the world. "Come out with me and the girls. They've been hounding me about getting you new clothes." He glanced at my outfit—jeans and one of my brother's Michigan hoodies—with a small smile.

"What, they're still on that?" I asked. "Seriously? Why?"

"Even they get bored of shopping just for themselves sometimes," he answered matter-of-factly.

"I don't want any new clothes," I said defensively, putting my hands in my hoodie's front pocket.

"You should." He took his eyes off the road for a long moment and looked me up and down again. "And you might after you hang with them. They're pretty convincing ladies." Camden grinned at me. "Tell you what. I'll buy you something. My retirement gift to you."

I pondered this. What the hell, I deserved a break for working so hard. "Okay," I said finally. "We'll celebrate my retirement."

"If I could make one request, though?" asked Camden. We were almost back to school, and he pulled the car over to the side of the road and looked at me. "Can you only semi-retire, and at least keep doing my homework?"

"Seriously?" I looked at him, surprised. "You actually care who does it?"

"Just the Algebra. The typed stuff can be whoever. I've gotten used to your handwriting." He shrugged.

"I thought you said my handwriting sucks," I said.

"I've gotten used to your sucking, then," he said. I raised an eyebrow at him, and he actually reached over with a finger and moved it back down. A second later, we both burst out laughing.

chapter twelve

It's the weirdest feeling when suddenly, people at school know who you are. If there were such a thing as paparazzi at Weston High, they'd have been following the likes of Camden and Derek and Stacey and Dani around, and eventually they would've started getting me, and eventually Jonny and Cat, in the corners of their shots. It started with that day I went to the mall with Camden, Stacey, and Dani. They insisted on dragging me into Bebe and A&F and not letting me anywhere *near* the sales rack, which is the only place I'll even look in stores that expensive, even though the sale stuff usually costs too much as well. Then Stacey and Dani shopped for themselves for a while, parking it in the middle of the Juniors section at Nordstrom and throwing on a succession of skimpy little tops over the tanks they were already wearing. Camden would then pass judgment—he pronounced most of the items "hot" on Dani and "sorta skanky" on Stacey . . . which was exactly what each of them was going for.

Finally, the three of them hauled me into Forever 21 and insisted I start trying things on. Fine, I'm not unfamiliar with the concept of the twelve-dollar fitted tee, but they had other ideas. I said no to the gold sequined deep V-neck tank, no to the pre-distressed skinny jeans, and *heck* no to the mini-est miniskirt I had ever seen in my life when Dani shoved it at me with a wicked smile . . . only to find it stuffed into my backpack later when I got home. There was a Post-it note with Camden's writing on it that said, *Your assignment tomorrow is to wear this. You will be paid $0.*

"Oh, for chrissakes," I said, taking it out of the bag, looking at it, and then putting it back in. I tossed the bag into a corner of my room, on top of my history books, and resolved to give the skirt back to Camden the next day so he could return it.

Later that night, I took it out of the bag again and tried it on. *Hmmm.* It was red and black, with a teeny-tiny houndstooth pattern just barely big enough to see, and it was so short that it actually made my legs look longer and made me look taller. I stared at myself in the mirror, surprised. It didn't look bad. It didn't look bad at all.

No. I took it off and put it away, resolving to forget about it. I couldn't wear a skirt like that. It totally wasn't me.

Who am I kidding? I totally wore it the next day, albeit with black tights. The damn thing looked great on me. I offered to pay Camden back, but he just waved me off, and after school that day I went shopping with Dani and Stacey again. I figured I could buy some stuff if I un-retired and did maybe *one* extra assignment, which would take me twenty minutes . . . which meant I would lose twenty minutes of sleep, but possibly gain a new wardrobe. Yeah, the trade-off was worth it.

Dani and Stacey were actually really easy to hang out with, because they spent most of the time talking to each other, so it wasn't like I had to worry about keeping up my end of any conversation. That afternoon, they spent half the time debating the relative merits of Stila Lip Glaze versus the Sephora store brand gloss (Stila, while more expensive, won because of its flavor), a third of the time gossiping about particularly sketchy school hookups ("Shut up, Derek's little sister and that hottie student teacher? What is he, like, twenty-two? Nuh-uh! Shut up! She's fifteen? Nuh-uh!"), and about two seconds debating their chances at getting into their top-choice colleges (Stacey's was Central Michigan; Dani's was Eastern—which surprised me, as I'd always thought that everyone wanted to get as far out of the state as possible, like I did). The rest of the time they spent wondering what my workout program was.

"Nothing," I said. I've never worked out a day in my life.

"But look at your arms," Dani said, stopping in the middle of the food court to pull my cardigan off of my shoulder and push my T-shirt sleeve up.

I looked at my arms. They looked the same as they always did. "I wait tables, so I carry a lot of plates and trays and stuff," I offered.

"Ohhh," said Stacey. "That's why they're so toned! Oh my God, maybe I should get a waitressing job! Then I can work out and make money at the same time!"

"But, Stacey, at the gym you can work out and *watch TV* at the same time," Dani said, flashing me an amused "Ain't she a character?" sort of glance. I giggled a little.

"Oh. Yeah!" Stacey brightened. "Oh my God, did you see last night's *Road Rules*?"

Of course Dani had seen it.

The next morning, Cat waved at me as she approached my locker, then stopped dead in her tracks, staring at me from six feet away. After a second, she started moving again, very slowly, and came all the way up to me, staring and frowning the whole way.

"What?" I asked.

She frantically gestured at my face, down to my toes,

and back up again. "Since when are you shopping at Pacific *Slut*wear?" she demanded.

"What? Not everything there is slutty," I said, self-consciously backing away a little.

Cat glanced down at my stomach, a half-inch sliver of which was showing beneath my shirt. "It is if you buy it in that size."

I yanked the shirt down. It immediately rode back up. "It shrank in the wash," I said defensively. It hadn't, of course—it was a brand-new, very cute (I thought) cap-sleeved baby tee, which I was particularly psyched to be wearing because it was warm enough today to ditch the whole cardigan, hoodie, or jacket thing, which had to be taken advantage of. I was expecting the Michigan spring to snap back to freezing at any point, like it almost always did at least once before finally succumbing to its own warmth.

Cat stared at me, unconvinced.

"Yeah, okay, fine, it didn't shrink. So sue me," I said. "You should come shopping with us next time," I added, trying to deflect her suspicion. If I got Cat in on the whole thing, she couldn't very well give me any grief for it.

"Who's *us*?" Cat asked.

"Uh . . . it's me, Dani, and Stacey?" I smiled a weak, hopeful smile.

"Ha!" She started laughing. "Seriously?"

"Seriously," I said, picking up my phone to text Sarah.

It couldn't hurt to invite her along too, and the thought of hanging out with my old friends and my new sort-of-friends all at the same time sounded pretty fun . . . well, as long as nobody talked about anything to do with homework cheating. "They're actually kinda good at picking out stuff you wouldn't normally wear but that ends up looking good—"

"Good to who?" Cat gestured down at her own outfit, which could most accurately be described as "Japanese cartoon Goth field hockey player plus, for some reason, a purple corduroy newsboy cap."

"Just come next time," I said, looking glumly at my phone—Sarah had texted back almost instantaneously with a polite, but cold, *No thx.* I looked up at Cat, hoping she'd be more agreeable. "Just come?" I repeated. "Then we'll have something to talk about besides *The Hills.*"

"I freaking love that show," said Cat.

"Well, then you're halfway there." Of course, halfway seemed to be about as far as it was going to get that day— Stacey and Dani, upon their first glance at Cat after school, immediately looked at each other and screamed, "Makeover!"

"Never," said Cat. There ended that discussion.

"What is Cat short for?" asked Dani.

"Catalina," said Cat.

"Ever think of going by Lina?" asked Stacey.

"Never," said Cat. There ended *that* discussion.

We still had fun shopping that day. Stacey and Dani were in full-on dress mode—Stacey needed something for Spring Fling, having already lined up what she was wearing to prom, and Dani had the opposite problem. They tried to rope me and Cat into their mania too, as they practically ripped apart the racks at Nordstrom and Macy's, and they looked absolutely flabbergasted when I told them that I wasn't going to either event (my parents were making me work the night of Spring Fling, and while I might have had a better shot at ditching my shift for prom, considering it was almost three months away, it wasn't like I had anyone to go with). Cat's excuse floored them even more—she *was* going, in a group to the Fling and with Jonny to prom, but she was wearing the same thing to both: a vintage dress she'd found at the Salvation Army for eight bucks.

"Salvation?" Stacey asked, clutching her purse in shock. She squeezed the metal clasp so hard the nail polish on one of her nails chipped off.

"Army?" Dani asked, pausing with her lip gloss wand halfway to her mouth.

"Yeah," Cat said, exchanging an amused glance with me. Neither of us could believe that they couldn't believe it.

"It's really pretty. I've seen it," I said, attempting to calm them down. "It's black lace, with sort of a scoop neck and a satin ribbon around the—"

Dani put up a hand, stopping me. "Dude, whatever

you need to tell yourself, but you don't need to tell us," she said melodramatically, then grinned. She finished applying her lip gloss and chucked it back in her bag, then looked around the section of Macy's where we were standing. "Forget this. We've looked at literally everything in here. Wanna take a drive to the outlets?"

I shook my head, feeling a small pang of guilt as I remembered that the last time I'd been outlet shopping was last summer with Sarah; her mom had driven us and we'd spent the entire afternoon trying things on and then ended up just buying two pairs of five-dollar flip-flops each. I wondered where she was at this exact moment—probably tutoring? Or at home doing her homework? "Can't," I told Dani. "I have to work like . . ." I checked my watch. "In like, an hour."

"Okay, then. Wanna go bikini shopping?"

I opened my mouth to say, "No way," but Stacey and Dani each took me by an arm and whisked me off to the swimwear department before I got a chance. Cat tagged along, smirking, and faster than you could say "hot tub"— although technically what was said was a rapid-fire "You need something to wear in the hot tub at Cam's house at his Spring Fling after-party, so shut up, we know you're not going to Spring Fling, but it doesn't mean you can't go to the after-party; now what do you want top-wise, halter or string? String it is. We know you didn't say anything, that was us deciding for you"—I found myself not only trying on a series of bikinis that my mother would have had me drawn and quartered for even looking at, but I actually found myself buying one of them: a simple, sporty little red number. It was no small investment at eighty-four dollars—in fact, it was a giant investment—but even I (and Cat, for that matter) had to admit that it looked really cute on me.

Camden was right—Dani and Stacey were some pretty convincing ladies indeed.

They eventually started hanging out with us at school, too, at least in the sense of saying hi in the hallway. Dani would stop me to chat about *American Idol*, or Stacey would ask me if her hair was looking okay (it always was). Sometimes Cat and I would run into them before lunch, and we'd walk to the cafeteria together, which meant there was never a shortage of guys staring right through me and Cat to Stacey's push-up bra or Dani's never-covered abs. Cat and I didn't mind—eventually we even stopped trading amused glances whenever it happened—and Jonny minded even less, especially when the girls occasionally started talking to him as well. I almost had a heart attack the first time I saw Stacey give him a little wave in the hallway—if they ever started talking about the homework ring and realized that there was a discrepancy in the amount of money being paid to and from, I was dead—but I had to trust that Camden had schooled our customers well in the art of shutting up, just as I had done with my friends. I just hoped that nobody ever accidentally let something slip out.

"You guys," Jonny said at lunch one day, puffing out his chest proudly as he sat down. "Dani Davis said hi to me today. It was *awesome*."

"Just because she said hi?" I asked.

"No, because she was below me on the stairs and I got a look down her shirt."

Cat and I laughed. Sarah didn't. "Wow. I guess that *would* be worth having to talk to her," she said, stabbing her salad viciously with a fork.

"Almost, yeah." Jonny cheerfully dug into his lunch as I sneaked a sideways glance at Sarah. She was still squarely in her "Don't ask, don't tell" mode regarding the home-work ring, but I'd never heard a tone that nasty coming out of her mouth before. Was it bothering her that Cat and I didn't hang out with her as much anymore? I'd invited her along on a few more Stacey and Dani shopping trips, but she always declined so quickly that I'd stopped bothering. Did she want me to start asking again? Was she happy that I wasn't?

I didn't have time to answer my own questions, because my phone beeped with a text from Dani, and Jonny imme-diately asked me if I could get her to come by our table and lean over it.

As for the business that had brought us together

in the first place, Camden and I were still trying to stay undercover whenever we were specifically discussing the homework operation, but after forgetting and saying hey to each other too many times in the hallway, we started giving up. And eventually, the rumor mill gave up too, now that the sight of us talking was so commonplace. After I became friendly with Dani and Stacey, it didn't take too long before Camden's guy friends were saying hey to me in the hallways too . . . and then hey to my friends . . . and then suddenly, one day, I saw people looking at me and Jonny and Cat when we were walking around together, and I realized that we'd somehow become some sort of weird offshoot of the popular crowd. People knew something was up; they just didn't know exactly what it was. They knew that we'd somehow managed to become cooler than we'd been a month ago; they just weren't sure why or how. I think Jonny put it best one morning when we were heading over to the tutoring office to check in with one of his students before a test: "You guys, if this were a movie, we'd all be walking in slow motion right now."

"We could do it anyway," Cat said, grinning. She made an elaborate show of deliberately slowing down her steps.

"Dork." I laughed, shoving her. "Besides, to do it right, we'd have to walk in slowly from around a corner while some badass song is playing, and they always do it with at least four people, so technically we've got it wrong."

"Too bad Sarah didn't want in," said Cat.

"Yeah," I said. "Too bad." I felt depressed for a split second, and started wondering where Sarah was . . . but then Brad Slater sneaked up behind me and yanked the ends of my hair. I turned around and smacked him, giggling as I did it, and was rewarded with a wink before he sauntered away.

"Whore," said Cat. I elbowed her. "Teach me," she added. I laughed.

Of course, there were difficulties in suddenly having ten times the social life I normally did. For one thing, there was explaining it to my parents. The new wardrobe items were easy to get past them without questions, because by the time they saw me every day I was usually about five seconds from changing, if not changed already, into my waitressing uniform of black pants, an apron, and my Pailin logo shirt. And they were used to losing track of me in between school and work, mostly because they always assumed I was tutoring or in the library. And the times they succumbed to their occasional fits of paranoia, well, that was where Camden's lying-to-your-parents-on-the-cell-phone training came in handy. Nat was so wrapped up in Star and his own stuff that the only time he appeared to notice was when he said, "Dude, you've been dressing kinda sluttier lately. Good for you." But the week that Camden invited me, and whoever else I wanted to bring, to swing by a party that Derek Rowe was having at his house, I realized there was no way I was going to be able to tell my parents the truth if I wanted to stay at the party any longer than half an hour.

"I'm sleeping over at your house," I told Cat that Saturday afternoon; I was calling her during a brief lull in the lunch shift action. "My parents are gonna drop me off at your house after work tonight."

"Are they gonna call the landline?" she asked.

"Almost certainly," I said. "Actually, maybe not . . . they've been going easier on me lately, probably because college letters are going out soon." It was nearly April, and my parents were just as nervous as I was about my chances of getting into Stanford, if not more so. "But we should probably operate as if they will, just in case," I added.

"Got it," Cat said. "Guess we'll just be fashionably late to this thing." Cat knew the drill—we couldn't leave for Derek's party until my parents called and made sure we were safely at her house. Luckily, they weren't so insane that they would physically drive over and check, so that Saturday night, once they called around eleven thirty—while both of us were watching TV and hovering right by the phone in order to grab it before it had a chance to wake Cat's parents—we got in her car, went to pick up Jonny, called Sarah one last time in case she'd changed her mind about going (she hadn't), and headed over to Derek's house. He lived in Camden's neighborhood, albeit on the slightly less fancy side of it (as in, the side of it closer to my own neighborhood), and we heard the party before we saw it—a faint thump of bass coming from nearly a block away, punctuated by lots of yelling and the occasional shriek of laughter. I saw Camden in the driveway, a shadowy figure with a beer in hand, as we parked behind a long, long, *long* line of cars on Derek's street.

"Yo, you made it . . . finally," Camden said as we approached. He was wearing jeans and a ratty blue striped polo shirt, making me feel slightly overdressed, even though I wasn't exactly rocking a particularly fancy look—just dark jeans and a sparkly green-and-gray striped tank top, under my new black, not quite cashmere but still really soft, sweater. I couldn't figure out if Camden's shirt was ratty because he'd bought it pre-distressed, or if it was actually something he genuinely wore a lot, but he somehow made it look good either way—the lighter stripes on the shirt matched his eyes. *Ugh*, there I was, noticing the eyes again.

"Jesus," I said, having to yell over the music, even though we weren't inside the house yet. "Are his parents not home?" I hesitated for a split second when Camden held out his beer to me, then thought, *Why not?* and grabbed it, taking a sip. *Yuck.*

"They're home," he said, grinning at the face I made at his beer as I handed it back to him. "They just don't care.

Go inside, guys," he said to Jonny and Cat, who were already halfway through the door. He then turned back to me. "So where's the bikini?" he asked. We were standing on the edge of Derek's giant front lawn; Camden drained the rest of his beer and then turned around and lobbed the empty can at the recycle bin sitting against the side of the garage. It *just* made it in. Impressive.

"What bikini?" I asked.

"Stacey and Dani said you guys went shopping and you got one," he said.

"They *made* me get one," I corrected.

"So you got one," he repeated.

"Technically true, yes." I allowed a small smile and flipped my hair back over my shoulders.

"Well, you know, Derek has a hot tub. I figured you might wear it. Is it underneath this?" Camden made a move for the edge of my tank top.

"Ha! In your dreams," I said, slapping his hand away.

"How did you know what I dream about?" he asked innocently, then looked me up and down, not as innocently. I felt my face turning red as my mind bounced back and forth between knowing exactly what he meant and trying to deny that I knew exactly what he meant. Thank God it was dark outside; the only light was coming from a few cracks in Derek's front hall curtains.

Camden smiled at me—he'd clearly noticed my

embarrassment, despite the bad lighting—and guided me toward the door. "Come on, the Jell-O shots await."

They didn't have to wait long. Granted, Jonny, Cat, and I had given ourselves a predetermined limit of two drinks each—none of us had been to a party with alcohol before, and we figured we should keep one another from becoming a teen movie cliché—but that didn't mean we didn't want to at least blend. The party spanned Derek's entire house, with the keg in the basement; an impromptu dance floor in the living room, with somebody using one of his hundreds of music channels to D.J. from the giant flat-screen TV; and Jell-O shots lining the entire kitchen island. The crowd was mostly kids from our school, juniors and seniors, but there were also a lot of kids from Greenbrook, the private school in town. I had no idea who any of them were, and could barely remember Camden's rapid-fire series of introductions— "This is Kelly, this is Aiden, this is Liz, this is Jeannette, this is Sam, this is other Sam . . ."—so I was *very* glad to have Cat and Jonny there, and vice versa. It seemed like they felt a little out of place despite the fun they were having, and so did I, so at least we always felt comfortable around one another. We circulated around the party with Stacey and Dani, and of course with Camden and his buddies, a little bit, but around two in the morning, the three of us were just kind of huddled in the corner of the living room on what was now a rather trashed-looking maroon leather couch, watching people dance drunkenly, make out drunkenly, make out while drunkenly dancing, or gradually fall asleep.

"Is it wrong that I sort of feel like drawing on Nate Rosenberg?" Jonny asked. Nate, who had taken Jonny's lunch money a couple different times in seventh and eighth grades, was passed out by the TV. One corner of Derek's Xbox was digging into his ribs. It looked painful.

"If you do it, I'll help you," Cat offered, digging into the side pocket of her bag for a pen. She found a black Sharpie and pulled the cap off of it with relish.

"I'm actually getting kinda tired," I said, stretching my neck and then stifling a yawn. "If you guys wanna leave—"

"Hey, smart chick! Dance with me!" said a voice, as a hand grabbed my arm and dragged me to my feet, then to the middle of the makeshift dance floor. The hand belonged to Dave Markley, whom I'd said hi to a handful of times and actually spoken with probably zero. I glanced back at Cat and Jonny, and they shrugged at me, then started debating between themselves whether to actually put Cat's Sharpie to use on Nate. Okay . . . nothing to do but break it down to Fergie, I guess.

"Damn, woman, you can move," Dave said, flailing his arms around and then leaning in really close to me;

his breath and striped button-down both reeked of beer. "That's something I never would've guessed about you."

"And you dance like a total white guy," I said, keeping my tone playful even as I tried to discreetly inch away. "Which I absolutely would have guessed about you."

"Oooh, smart chick, you're gonna pay for that!" Dave grabbed me in a ballroom dance grip and dipped me back dramatically, almost so my head touched the floor, before swinging me back up and twirling me around. Okay, despite the beer breath, that was kind of fun.

I was in the middle of laughing hysterically when I heard Camden's voice saying, "Now, is that any way to treat a lady?" He had appeared out of nowhere and was standing next to us, eyebrows raised at Dave.

"Dude, I'm kinda wasted. I don't know," said Dave. He draped his arm over me, mostly to hold himself up, and I staggered under the weight.

"I'm fine," I said to Camden. "My head actually cleared the floor by like, half an inch there, so I'm totally fine. . . ." It didn't matter—Camden had already latched on to my arm and was ushering me away from Dave. It was probably a good idea, because Dave looked like he was about to fall down—he had wandered off to the side and was literally leaning against the wall at this point, his cheek buried against Derek's living room drapes—but on the other hand, it wasn't like I couldn't have done a perfectly good job of rescuing myself if I'd felt the need to. I turned to Camden as we crossed into the kitchen and gave him a playful bump in the chest with my shoulder.

"Jealous?" I teased, looking up at him.

"Completely," he said. And I couldn't breathe for a second, because for the first time, he wasn't smirking.

chapter thirteen

"Okay, so Lara O'Connor needs an A on the history thing
so fifty-buck surcharge there . . . okay, and—wait, will you
have time to—"

"No problem, Bella will handle it."

"Cool, and Derek and I both have this stupid Chem
lab thing—"

"Jonny's on it. It can suck, right?"

"Duh. What else? Anything else besides the usual?"

"Nope. Nate still hasn't paid for last week, so you
should—"

"Oh, yeah, he gave me like, ten of his old Xbox games,
so I'm just gonna—"

"Oh, you're gonna cover it? Okay then, that's it for
today."

"Sweet."

"Sweet."

It was early April. As had become our routine, Camden and I were in his car after school; he was giving me a ride to work after I dropped off the day's assignments with our "employees" at the tutoring office, which provided me with, well, a free ride to work, as well as providing both of us with a spy-free environment in which to discuss whatever we needed to discuss, business-wise. It also made the cash handoffs a lot less sketchy—the stares we got in the hallways the first few times that envelopes changed hands made me feel hilariously like a drug dealer, but after a while, paranoia won out over amusement. Now, we were very careful not to arouse any suspicion; people still wondered how we had become friends, but once Angel Redford got pregnant and decided to have the baby, and then found out that baby turned out to be twins, the rumors starting focusing elsewhere. Thanks, easily distracted high school students! And thanks, Angel and her boyfriend's laissez-faire attitude toward condoms.

"Here's good," I said, as Camden pulled up to the little driveway around the corner from our restaurant; it was on the way from the bus stop, so if my parents were bothering to look, it would seem like I'd still come from that direction. A few days a week, Nat and I were on the same schedule, so he'd raised an eyebrow the first day he saw me get into Camden's car instead of riding the bus, but all I had to do was mouth, "Star," at him, and I knew he wasn't going to be mentioning anything to our parents, accidentally or other-wise. I walked over to the mailbox and opened it as Camden started turning his car around to go home . . . and then stopped dead in my tracks and gasped when I saw what was in the mail.

"What?" Camden asked through his car window. He craned his neck to see what I was holding.

"Letter from Stanford," I said, my hands shaking. I could barely get the words out. *Please let this be an accep-tance. Please let this be an acceptance.*

"That thing's pretty big," Camden pointed out. "You probably got—"

"Shut up!" I squeaked, unwilling to jinx anything by making assumptions. I shrugged my backpack off and let it drop to the ground, then closed my eyes and clum-sily opened the envelope blind. I pulled the contents out, nearly giving myself a paper cut, and then opened my eyes again. "We are pleased to inform you . . . *Aaaaaahhhhhh!!!*" I screamed.

"Christ, what the hell?" asked Camden. He'd left his car idling and had gotten out, and was now standing next to me.

"I got in!" I whooped. "I got in!" I jumped up and down, laughed hysterically in delight for a few seconds, and then, impulsively, I threw my arms around Camden's neck and hugged him.

He let me.

And after a few moments, he gently took my face in his hands and kissed me.

I let him.

It went on for a while, which either surprised the hell out of both of us or didn't surprise us at all. I didn't really know; I was too busy not thinking.

"Uh," I said, finally pulling away. "Sorry about, uh . . . or, I mean, not sorry. Or . . . I didn't mean to—"

"Shut up," he said, his hands now on my waist. "And congratulations."

"Thanks," I laughed. It occurred to me that I might want to take a look around and see if Nat or anyone else was looking at us, but for some reason I couldn't tear my eyes off of Camden's face.

"So this means you're headed pretty far away next year, huh?" he asked.

"You're damn right I am," I answered with satisfaction. *California, here I come!*

"Bummer," he said, and it sounded like he meant it. He looked at me steadily with those blue, blue eyes. I looked back at him. It was silent for a moment.

"Anyway," I finally said, as the comfortable silence started to edge up on uncomfortable. "So, uh, I should probably get to work."

"Probably," he agreed, nodding slightly. I tried to take

a step back but couldn't; he'd purposely tightened his arms around me.

"It'd be easier if you'd let go," I pointed out. Not that I should've been talking—I was the one standing on my tip-toes to be closer to him.

His witty comeback was to kiss me again.

"Okay, seriously," I said, disentangling myself a few moments later. "Work. Is there. Waiting for me. To also be there." Had I suddenly developed asthma? I could barely breathe . . . except that I knew I must be breathing, because I could smell the clean, soapy scent of Camden's hair and skin, and the pleasant detergent smell on his clothes . . .

"Okay, okay," Camden said, stepping away from me slowly, his hands lingering on my waist, then my hair, before he finally backed off fully. He got back in his car. "See ya tomorrow." He smiled at me, holding my gaze for several seconds before hitting the gas pedal and driving off.

"Okay, 'bye," I said, my stomach doing jumping jacks. I watched his car disappear down the street as I bent over and picked up my Stanford acceptance, and the rest of the mail, off the ground from where it had fallen when I'd thrown my arms around Camden. I started reading the letter again and leafing through the information booklet that came with it, basking in the glow of having my future all settled while simultaneously trying to shut down the little voice in my head asking me, *Did you just add yourself to the looong list of Camden King conquests? Did you just sign yourself up for getting totally screwed over?* My God, had I? Whatever, I'd just gotten into Stanford—I should be thinking about sunshine and redwood trees and mild winters, not anything else, and I certainly shouldn't be worrying. But this kiss had been . . . it had been so . . . oh man, what was he going to say about me at school the next day? Anything? Nothing? Was he going to pretend it had never happened? Should *I* pretend it had never happened?

My phone beeped with a text. *BTW I xpect a discount on tonights hw. :)* Okay, he clearly wasn't pretending it had never happened. I smiled at the text, then frowned. Wait a minute, what did he mean? Was this a good thing or a bad thing? He wasn't serious, was he? I couldn't figure it out. Time for a lighthearted, noncommittal answer. I was in the middle of texting back, *In your dreams,* when, from out of nowhere, Leonard appeared behind me.

"You probably just contracted herpes," he said.

"Oh my God!" I jumped, nearly dropping my phone. "What the—how long have you been there?"

"As they often say in these situations, long enough." Leonard put his hands in his pockets and leaned back against the outside wall of the restaurant, staring at me coolly through his glasses.

"Did you *follow* me?" I asked. I looked around frantically, trying to figure out where he'd been hiding.

"Not technically. It's not like I didn't know you work here. I just showed up where I knew you'd be." He rocked back and forth on his feet, looking a little bit shifty and a lot self-satisfied.

"Well, what's up?" I asked, trying to sound chipper. So he'd caught me making out with Camden. That meant that it would definitely be all over school by tomorrow morning, but whatever, maybe it wasn't a big deal. Oh my God, no. It *was* a big deal. Would people think we were dating? Had he hooked up with anyone else lately? Would he deny it all? Should *I* deny it all? A flood of questions about Camden rushed into my head, and I struggled not to think about them. I had to calm down.

"I know you're doing people's homework for money," Leonard said.

Nope. I had to panic.

"What? No, I'm not," I said. My voice cracked on the word *not*.

"Oh, right, you're not anymore. You've got other people doing it for you," he said. He crossed his arms and grinned an evil little grin at me.

Oh my God.

I didn't say anything further, just clasped my cell and the mail I was holding tightly to my chest and waited to see what was about to happen—I knew it wasn't going to be good, so I wasn't about to speed it up. Trying not to throw up, or faint, or let my face shift from the carefully neutral expression I currently had pasted onto it, I listened as Leonard detailed what he knew about the cheating operation—which, somehow, was almost everything.

"So that about covers it," Leonard said finally, and very cheerfully. "Man," he added, "if you'd just told me about this weeks ago, this could've all gone down so differently. Oh, and by the way, Maya . . . it's one thing to cheat in school. I mean, you might get expelled, which already sucks. But then you go for *that* guy? Do you know where he's *been*? He uses girls and chucks them out. I thought you were smarter than that."

I felt my whole body turn to ice. He was obviously lashing out partly because he was jealous—that was undeniable—but there was also truth to what he was saying. Hell, I'd gone to school with Camden for almost three years and had witnessed it myself—but I wasn't about to let Leonard see me cringe.

"What do you want?" I asked coldly. "Do you want in? Because we can always use more people—"

"Oh, so *now* you start being nice?" he snapped, before turning on a dime to smile at me. "Actually, that's exactly what I wanted—for you to be nice. But I wasn't thinking so much in terms of you inviting me in on your little scheme. You guys are gonna go down eventually, and I'm not messing up my perfect record to go down with you. I was thinking"—he paused dramatically—"more along the lines of you being my date to the Spring Fling. And your prom," he added for good measure.

"What? No way!" I said automatically, backing away from him with a grossed-out twitch of my shoulders. Then I caught the look of hurt that flashed across his face and instantly regretted it. Leonard narrowed his eyes.

"Well, if you don't want to buy my silence that way," he said, "then you'll just have to buy it with cash." He uncrossed his arms and shook them out for a moment, then crossed them again. "I'll take five thousand to start."

My eyes widened as I felt my throat close in fear. "Are you blackmailing me?" I whispered.

"Well, you do seem to like guys with money," he answered icily.

I stared at him, furious that he would dare to suggest that I only liked Camden for his money, more furious at myself for just admitting in my own head that I liked Camden, and deathly, deathly afraid of what my life was about to become. I tried to form words, any words; I tried to form my hand into a fist; I pondered picking up my backpack, with its load of heavy books, off the ground and clocking him with it. I was completely unable to do any of those things.

Leonard, tired of waiting for me to react, shrugged and stood up straight. "You've got two weeks to pay me. And then, I tell the principal," he said, turning around and starting to trudge in the direction of the bus stop. I watched him go, still completely unable to move. My feet were stuck in place on the sidewalk, even though the wind had started up and was in the process of turning a pleasant spring afternoon into a chilly one.

I stood there for what seemed like a long time.

Nat came around the corner, dressed in his Pailin shirt and apron. "Dude, what's taking you so long?" he asked, then saw the envelope from Stanford in my hand and the stricken look on my face. "Are you okay? Oh no, did you get rejected?" He took the letter out of my hand and read it, as I suddenly remembered that ten minutes ago I had been kissing a hot, if sketchy, guy and celebrating getting into my dream school. Oh, how quickly things change.

"Dude, you got in!" Nat whooped, shoving my shoulder so hard that I almost fell over. "That is awesome!"

"What?" I asked. "Oh, yeah. Totally. Sorry. I think, I think I was just, uh, in shock," I stammered. I cast my gaze downward, to avoid catching his eye, and saw that my hand was still clutching my cell phone so tightly that my knuckles were white. For a moment I dimly remembered that Sarah must've gotten her letter too, and I wondered if I should call her to see if she'd also gotten in, but the thought slipped from my mind as I remembered Leonard's words.

"Well, get out of it. You gotta tell Mom and Dad!" Nat gathered up my stuff and the rest of the mail, then dragged me and my acceptance letter into the restaurant and, ignoring the fact that there was already an extremely early pair of diners chilling at Table Two, ran up to my mom at the cash register and shoved the letter in her face. Her eyes lit up and she joyfully covered her mouth with her hand as Nat ran back to the kitchen to get my dad, and before I knew it, my parents, Nat, Krai, and the two random customers formerly sitting at Table Two were surrounding me, yelling various forms of congratulations and toasting one another with freshly opened bottles of Singha beer. My mom doesn't even drink beer, and she was drinking beer, and while I was doing my best to smile and look totally psyched—and a tiny part of me *was* totally psyched—most of me was about three seconds away from absolute hysteria.

"Hopefully we do good business tonight," my mom joked, looking around the room and beaming. "We've got Maya's Stanford tuition to pay!" She and my dad merrily clinked beer bottles, and my dad actually took his baseball cap off and threw it in the air, and suddenly the hysteria hit. *Aaah!* Everything I had been doing was to pay off that fine. I was already killing myself just to keep the restaurant afloat, and now, because of that stupid little punk Leonard ... *argh! Now* what? What was I going to do? We were already doing work for all of Camden's friends, and even his giant social circle had finite edges. How was I suddenly going to make the extra five grand? How did I know

Leonard wouldn't turn us in anyway? I had been planning on stopping all of this madness the very second the fine was paid off, but what if Leonard kept on asking for money? Was I going to have to do this for the rest of the year, just in order to keep him quiet? Was I going to have to do this *forever*? Christ! What the *hell* was I going to do?

Well, step one was to tell Camden. I excused myself, leaving my family to their laughter and celebration, and went to the employee bathroom, locking the door and quickly splashing some water onto my face. I then took my phone from my pocket and restarted the text message to Camden that I'd begun almost an hour ago. I punched the clear button, erasing what I'd typed before. The new text: *We r *DEAD.**

chapter fourteen

I didn't run into Camden at all the next day at school, which was just as well because almost every class began with people asking "Where'd you get in?" and then, depending on the situation, reactions of ecstasy or anguish. It was mostly ecstasy for my friends—Sarah, Cat, and Jonny had all gotten into their first choices of Stanford, Brown, and M.I.T., respectively—but, as people congratulated me on my own Stanford acceptance, the most I could muster was a weak smile. I had bigger things to think about—much, much bigger things.

I'd tried to explain the Leonard story to Camden in a frenzy of late-night texting after I'd gotten home from work, but had given up after my fingers cramped. The last text I saw before drifting off into a panicky, nightmare-filled sleep (in which an eight-foot-tall Leonard with vampire teeth sucked both my parents dry before taking me to the prom and somehow orchestrating it so that my dress suddenly became transparent) was *Dont worry c u at car 2morrow. Everything will be fine.* I wished I could believe him.

I met Camden at his car after school and the first thing he did was wrap his arms around me and bend down to give me a quick kiss. That made me feel a little better. Until, after realizing that half the crew team had seen us and were elbowing one another going, "Oh, dude, WHAT?" I felt slightly worse. But there wasn't any time to worry about stuff like that. The mystery of whether I'd somehow managed to acquire a hookup partner (maybe?) or a boyfriend (possibly?) was big, as was my sudden desire to find out whether or not Camden was still taking Dani to the Spring Fling, but the Leonard problem was bigger. Way bigger.

Camden and I got in his car, and he pulled out of the parking lot and started driving randomly as usual. "Okay," I said, struggling to keep my voice calm. "Here's why we're completely and totally screwed."

I told him what had happened yesterday with Leonard. He'd managed to sort of glean part of it from my panicky texts, but most of it he hadn't, and when I got to the part with the word *blackmail,* he slammed on the brakes, hard and angrily.

"WHAT?" he yelled. Behind us, two more cars screeched on their brakes in order to avoid rear-ending Camden's Escalade. There was a frenzy of horn honking, and I scrunched down in my seat as Camden reached his left hand out his window and flipped off everyone behind us. After a moment, he put his foot on the gas pedal and got us going again, then changed his mind and let the car drift onto the side of the street and come to a stop.

I finished the story as calmly and quickly as I could, watching as Camden's grip on the steering wheel grew tighter and tighter.

"Christ," he said when I was done. He finally let go of the steering wheel, shaking out his hands. "Well, that's easy. I'll just kick that kid's butt." He shook out his hands some more and then started cracking his knuckles.

"You can't do that," I said. "If you do, he'll tell the principal right away and then we'll *really* be screwed."

"He can't tell anybody if I break his jaw."

"He could write it down."

"And his hands."

"They could hook him up to one of those eye scanner things."

"Fine, I'll just kill him. Can't be too hard. Derek and Brad could help. And Dani. She's got a serious vicious streak." He leaned to the side in order to grab his cell phone out of his pocket.

"Camden . . ." I said.

"Seriously, this one time back when we were dating,

this other chick was kinda flirting with me, and Dani took her nail file and—"

"Camden!" I said.

"I know, I know, not helping. Sorry," he said. He agitatedly drummed his fingers on the steering wheel, then started up the car again and slammed on the gas with a vengeance, screeching us forward into traffic and nearly clipping a passing Jetta. Another lengthy horn honk was sent in our direction, provoking another lengthy show of Camden's middle finger to the world at large. "Okay, look," he said, pulling his hand back into the car and accelerating until we were going a good fifteen miles above the speed limit. "I'll just ask my parents for the money."

I emphatically shook my head. "No. No way. You can't ask them for five grand!"

"Sure I can. I doubt they'll give it to me unless I come up with a *really* good lie, but it's worth a shot." He pulled into a side street and stopped the car again; this time we were parked in front of a random house.

"I can't take your parents' money," I said. "I mean, for one thing, I just can't, and for another, do you know how long it would take me to pay them back?"

"You wouldn't have to pay them back," Camden shrugged, then, glancing over and catching the look on my face, he repeated it more emphatically. "You wouldn't!"

I turned to look at him, then reached out and moved his face so that instead of staring out the front window, he was looking directly into my eyes. "Camden. I'd have to pay them back."

He sighed. "Fine. I'll steal it from them, then you can owe me instead. And I'll let you work it off in sex." He smirked at me. "I'm only half kidding."

"And at any other time I might've found that half funny," I snapped, "but right now, I'm too busy *panicking!*" I threw my head back against the headrest, covering my eyes with my hands and taking a deep breath.

"Hey. *Hey*," said Camden. "Everything's gonna be fine, okay?" He reached toward me and gently started to move a lock of my hair behind my ear.

"Maybe for you," I said, smacking his hand away. "Some of us are gonna be living out the rest of our lives in a rice paddy wearing a big hat."

"Wow, you get racist when you're panicky."

"Shut your pathetic, useless mouth."

"And bitchy."

I was bored of having my head back. I slammed it forward onto the dashboard instead.

"Okay, look," Camden said, his voice now calm and logical. "We just have to figure out a way to make the extra money. That's all. Let's not worry about anything else right now, okay? Let's not overthink it. We're just gonna figure out a way to make five grand in two weeks. Got it?" He studied me, his face encouraging.

I took a deep breath, then let it out. "Got it."

"How much money do you have in your bank account?"

"Don't have one," I said. "How much do you have in yours?"

"Uh . . . not so much," he answered.

I looked up at him, surprised. "Isn't your allowance like, a couple hundred a week?"

"Dude, I *spend* that," Camden said, giving me a "duh" glance. I opened my mouth a little in disbelief, and he glared at me.

We sat in silence for a while.

"I've got it," he said suddenly. "We rob a bank."

It was my turn to glare at him.

"Hey, they're not all gonna be winners," he said matter-of-factly. "Just trying to keep the juices flowing here."

I sighed. "You know, I almost wish that all the teachers at school would suddenly go nuts and assign twice as much homework. I mean, we're pretty much doing every single assignment for every single kid at our school who can afford it right now, but if they suddenly had more work—"

"Huh," Camden said thoughtfully. "Well, we can always get more work."

"No, we're pretty much maxed out. That's the whole thing. That's what I just said."

"No, we aren't." Camden was beginning to sit up a little straighter. "We're not the only school in town." He looked like the wheels were beginning to turn in his head.

"Wait, do you think you know enough people at other schools?" I asked.

"Of course," he said, sounding excited now. "I went to Greenbrook for a semester, remember? Before I got thrown out."

"What for?" I raised an eyebrow.

He grinned at me. "Cheating."

Figured. I put my head back down on the dashboard as he started up the car again; it was almost time for my shift, and I needed to put on my happy waitress face . . . or at least take off my stressed-out, "I hate Leonard" face.

"Dude, that's it, though," Camden said, tapping his fingers on the steering wheel and speeding on his way to the restaurant. "That's it, that's perfect. Give me a few days and I guarantee you I can round up some clients from Greenbrook. Then all you have to do is make sure you have enough people to do the work."

"Oh, I'll have enough people," I said. "I'll do it myself and not sleep for the next two weeks if I have to." I heard the edge in my own voice and I knew he heard it too—I meant it.

"Okay, then. Well, that's what we're gonna do."

"Okay," I said.

"Good," he said.

"Good," I repeated. We were at the restaurant, parked around the corner as usual. I made a move to get out of the car and he hit the automatic door locks on me.

"Nice try," he said, grabbing the edge of my jacket and pulling me into a kiss.

Well, I thought, melting into his arms and breathing in the now familiar clean scent of his hair, *if I'm gonna get expelled for cheating and go to hell for screwing over my parents and friends, I might as well have a good time on the way.*

I spent most of the next day wondering how much to tell the other people in the cheating ring about why we were suddenly expanding (I decided on as little as possible), and worrying what would happen if they were all happy with the amount of money they were already making and didn't feel like doing any more work (I was only able to put that scary thought out of my mind sometime toward the end of fifth period, when the fire alarm went off and we all had to evacuate for half an hour, even though it turned out to be some burned popcorn in the teachers' lounge microwave). I texted everyone and told them to meet me in the library after school. With just over two weeks until I had to pay both the Health Department and Leonard, this operation needed to be kicked up a notch A.S.A.P. Hopefully, if we went into one of the study rooms, we would just look like a study group. A huge one. A huge one where, for some reason, everybody was in different grades and carrying different books.

Sigh.

After school, our cheating ring employees—Cat, Jonny, their sisters Bella and Jill, and Bella's friends and Science Olympiad teammates Darren and Lucas—gradually filtered into one of the library's study rooms in the back corner, with a big, rectangular table and a few uncomfortable wooden "Don't you dare fall asleep here" chairs. Feeling weirdly like a gang leader, I took a suspicious look around the library to make sure that nobody was paying attention to us, then stepped inside and shut the door, sat down at the head of the table, and explained the bare-bones cover story I'd decided to give—that there was a *lot* of money to be had because private school kids were even richer than the rich kids at our school, and that therefore we could charge them even more for the same stuff. And while it would suck for the next few weeks because I was expecting Camden to have rounded up a *lot* of clients, hey, it was worth it to try it out, right? I barely avoided saying a perky "So, who's with me?" at the end of what I hoped was a rousing speech. Instead I just sat there, fiddling with my sleeves and waiting to see what would happen.

"Eh," Cat said, taking off the nonprescription red glasses she was wearing and setting them down on the table with a click. "That sounds like it might sort of negate the whole 'easy money' selling point of this entire thing. I mean, if it's really that much work—"

"I know, I know," I said, forcing myself to sound casual. "Just . . . everyone think about it, okay? Honestly, I don't even know how many clients we're gonna have yet, but just remember, most of the papers won't have to be any good, so it'll probably take less time than you think. And if they do have to be good, well, we charge extra for that." I looked around at a table full of skeptical faces. "A lot extra," I added. "Remember, they're rich private school kids." I scribbled a note that said, *And their rich private PARTAYS*, and shoved it in front of Cat and Jonny. They read it, and Jonny cracked a smile as Cat looked up at me and grinned.

"Point taken," she mouthed. She was enjoying her new cheating ring–created social life as much as, or more than, anyone.

There was a lot of murmuring as everyone gathered up their stuff to leave, and I forced myself not to hiss, "Murmur quieter!" at they wandered toward the door. The paranoia that people were going to find out was growing on me as the group grew, and I didn't know what I was going to do if any information filtered out. Would I deny everything? Bring each new person into the circle? I watched everyone leave as

Cat, Jonny, and Bella deliberately lagged behind. As soon as the door swung shut, they pounced.

"Dude, how come you *really* decided to expand?" Jonny asked, leaning back against the door and crossing his arms. He stared at me through his glasses.

"Every business expands eventually." I shrugged. I'd figured this was coming, and it wasn't too hard to keep my tone nonchalant. "Those private school kids are totally used to having everything done for them; why not take advantage of it? It's term paper season—we could make a killing."

"Well, yeah," Jonny said, "but it sounds like we might not be able to keep up with demand. If Camden really knows that many people—"

"We'll keep up," I said quickly. "Hell, it's not like we can't find more people if necessary."

"My boyfriend would probably do it," offered Bella.

"Joe's an idiot," said Cat.

"What's your point?" Bella asked flatly.

"That you've got bad taste in—"

"Hey," I said, before they could start one of their patented sisterly squabbles. "You know who's really good at writing papers really fast?"

Jonny and Cat looked at each other, and then at me. "Oh no," Cat said. "You can't. Not again."

"But she could totally help," I said. I couldn't keep from sounding a little wistful—Sarah's been known to write a ten-page English paper, complete with correct citations, in an hour . . . and get an A+ on it. If she were to get in on the deal, that would mean more money, and faster. And what with being able to charge more for A papers, it would mean more money, exponentially faster.

"You know she won't do it," Jonny said, shaking his head. "You've already tried like, a zillion times."

"If at first you don't succeed," I said, picking up my backpack and slinging it over my shoulders. Sarah was probably in the tutoring office right now; no time like the present.

"Or at second, or at third," Cat said, backing up Jonny. "Dude, don't bother asking her. It's like Tara Reid's comeback—it's just not gonna happen."

"Never say never," I said, pushing my way out the door. After all, Sarah had said no before because she thought we were just being shady and doing it for the money—I hadn't tried telling her the truth yet. Maybe if I did, she would agree to help. We'd been friends since before either of us could even spell the word *friends*. She'd help bail me out, right? Even if she thought it was wrong? Even if we hadn't exactly been hanging out as much lately? She'd do it if she knew that my family's restaurant and our whole future together at Stanford were on the line, right?

I found Sarah in the tutoring office, doing her homework on the couch in the main room.

"Hey," I said.

"Hey," she said, looking up at me in surprise. "What's up?"

There were a few people putting together some sort of biology presentation on a foam board at the big table, so I dragged her into one of the study rooms, came back out and got all her stuff and dragged it all in too, shut the door, pulled down the blinds, and spilled the entire story—the fine, the cheating ring, the blackmail, everything. She listened quietly, her eyes widening and widening, right up until I said, "So. I'm begging you. Do you think you could help us out, just for the next two weeks? Nobody can write a paper faster than you."

"Hmmm," she said. Her tone was completely neutral. "Does anyone else know about this blackmail develop-ment?" Sarah reached back to tighten her ponytail, then leaned toward me, putting her elbows on the table and propping her chin on her hands.

"No," I said, nervously starting to twirl a pencil with my right hand while twisting a lock of hair with my left. "I didn't tell anyone except you and Camden."

Sarah's eyes narrowed slightly at the mention of his name. "So, along with the cheating, you're also lying to Jonny and Cat and most of our other friends?" she asked. So much for her previous neutrality. By the end of the sen-tence, her normally soft voice had developed an unpleasant edge to it.

"Uh . . . I guess," I said, shifting uncomfortably in my chair. This was not exactly going the way I'd envisioned it. I debated explaining to her that the whole reason I was even telling her the whole story now was that I trusted her more than I trusted Cat and Jonny . . . not that I thought they would tell, necessarily, but . . . Sarah's voice cut off my train of thought.

"And you expect me to first of all be okay with that, and second of all bail you out even though you've barely talked to me the last couple of weeks?" The softness in her voice had now completely disappeared and her entire body was weirdly still. "By the way," she said pointedly. "Did you get into Stanford?"

Oh my God. How had we not talked about that yet?

The pencil I was twirling in my fingers slipped out of my hand and clattered noisily across the table. "Uh, yeah," I said, avoiding her eyes. "Did . . . did you?" I knew the answer, but I was sure she'd known my answer too. She was just making a point.

"Yeah," she said icily.

I suddenly realized that not only had she and I not talked about Stanford yet, we hadn't talked about *anything* lately, because my head had been totally distracted the last few weeks, and certainly the last two days—I had been panicky over Leonard's blackmail, fearful about paying the Health Department fine in time, and brimming with a mixture of anxiety, happiness, nervousness, and giddiness over everything that was going on with Camden. Christ, I hadn't even talked to her about Camden; she hated him, but I could have tried, at least. My God, I was losing it. I was a terrible person.

"Sarah," I started, not sure of what I was about to say, but certain that I had to turn this around somehow or else I was going to lose my best friend, along with everything else. "I'm sorry. I know we . . . I mean, I wouldn't have . . . I mean—" I didn't get any further than that because there was a tap on the window and then, without any pause at all, the door swung open and Leonard poked his head inside. I glared at him.

"What the hell do you want?" I snapped.

"Just wanted to see how you're doing," he said innocently. "Hi, Sarah," he added, giving her a little wave. She ignored him.

"Fine," I said through clenched teeth.

"And how's your boyfriend?" he went on. Sarah whipped her head around to look at me.

"He's not my—he's fine too," I said, my hands curled into fists under the table. "Anything else?"

"Nope!" Leonard jauntily adjusted his baseball cap, taking it off, bending the brim, and then putting it on again backward. "Well, good luck with *everything* that's going on in your life right now, Maya. 'Bye, Sarah." Leonard gave us another cheerful wave and left, shutting the door just hard enough to make the blinds swing a little. Sarah was still staring at me.

"So he's your boyfriend now?" she asked quietly.

"Uh . . . yes? No. I don't know. . . ."

"I can't believe you." Sarah shook her head and then started throwing her books and folders and papers into her bag without even closing the notebooks; everything was getting bent and crumpled and she didn't seem to care. "You've been so shady lately, and I want to think it's because you're just trying to pay off this fine—I mean, I can see where you *might* feel like you had to start this whole cheating thing. I feel bad for your parents too, but . . . hanging out with *him*? *That* guy? And his friends? The people who used to make fun of us? Who used to beat up your little brother?"

I winced; it was years ago, but it was true. Sarah noticed, and it fueled her fire; her eyes narrowed and her pale skin started growing pink. "I mean, do you not remember—do you realize what this *looks* like? Do you realize what people are gonna say? What they've probably *been* saying? About you? And him? Camden King-of-the-School has already done all the popular chicks, so he's branching out now."

"Okay, first of all—" I started.

"How could you let him talk you into this?" She was standing now, pacing back and forth on her side of the table.

"He didn't talk me into it," I said. "I'm the one who—"

"You never would've done this if it weren't for him, and now look what you've gotten yourself into!"

"I know," I said, trying to keep my voice calm so that at least one of us would be. "I didn't think it was gonna get this bad."

"Well, *I* did!" she exploded, the loudest I'd ever heard her yell, ever. "I *told* you so!"

I scooched back in my chair, crossing my arms, a little angry now. "Okay, I know that, but can we get past that and maybe focus on fixing the—"

"No, Maya, I'm not gonna get past it!" Sarah's face was now bright red. "You brought all of this on yourself, and worse, you let a total douche bag talk you into making it a huge train wreck instead of just telling the truth in the first place! He's using you, Maya! He's been using you this entire time and you were dumb enough to fall for it! And now you've been dressing like a slut—"

"I don't dress like a slut!"

"—just because he told you to—"

"He didn't tell me to do anything!"

"—and now you're gonna get yourself expelled and we're not gonna be able to go to Stanford together and you did it all just because of a *guy*, a *stupid, shallow, sketchpad* of a guy, and—"

"You're just jealous because a guy like him is into

me!" I yelled, my voice even louder than hers. "You're mad because I've actually got a life now, and you still don't, and I'm dating, and you never have!" I saw her face fall, and my stomach instantly knotted up, but I kept going anyway—I couldn't stop myself. I stood up, kicking my chair aside with a loud scraping noise, and swung my backpack onto my shoulder, glaring daggers at her. "If you don't wanna help me, fine. But I don't have to sit here and listen to all of your pathetic, childish, jealous crap!"

I got up and flung open the study room door, turning around for a moment to glare at her again. I could see that she was about to start crying, and as I walked through the doorway, I knew I already was.

I slammed the door anyway.

chapter fifteen

For getting your mind off a big problem, there's nothing
like a bigger problem. Sarah and I were now officially not
speaking—or at least, neither one of us was willing to see
if the other would talk, so that was pretty much the same
difference—but it wasn't like I was going to have the time
to talk to her anyway. If Camden and I were going to make
an extra five grand in the next two weeks, I was going to
have to come out of retirement; skimming off the top of
everybody else's assignments would help, but I was definitely going to have to supplement it with my own work.
Of course, that was assuming that Camden had managed to
round up enough clients from Greenbrook. I tried to hold
in the urge to ask him every two hours how the rainmaking
was going—the result being that I asked him every two
hours how the rainmaking was going.

"Dude," he finally said, tracking me down on Friday

morning in between second and third periods and yanking me into the Chem lab. "You can stop texting me. I'm working on it, okay? There's this chick, Kelly, I used to date over there. I hung out with her yesterday while you were at work and sort of started feeling things out. Just chill, okay? Everything will be fine." He reached out to give my hair a reassuring stroke, his fingers twining gently through the long strands.

"All right, all right. I was just wondering," I said, absently reaching out and hitching my fingers through one of the belt loops on his jeans. Great. His connection was the ex-girlfriend. And he was "feeling things out" with her. I remembered Sarah's words (and even my own, from a few weeks ago) about Camden's sketchy past, and paranoia rose up in my stomach. With a huge effort, I squashed it back down again and put a neutral expression on my face. "So . . . do you think Kelly will come through?" I asked cheerfully.

"Of course. She knows everyone. I'll have something by tomorrow at the latest, but if you're that worried about it, I could distract you 'til then."

"Yeah? With what?" I asked.

He grinned and leaned toward me until my back was pressed up against an old jazz choir audition poster.

Oh, right. That.

Well, shucks. Why not? A girl could use a good distraction every now and then.

By the end of the day, when I got in his car, Camden had the Greenbrook client list.

"Ta da," he said, tossing a few sheets of legal paper into my lap as he started up the car and gunned us out of the parking lot.

"Oh my God," I said, shifting in my seat and glancing through them. There had to be at least forty names, and he had put asterisks by the ones who had major term papers coming up—which was nearly everybody. So over the next two weeks, if they all had an average of one or two papers plus miscellaneous homework . . . yeah, it was doable. There would have to be some premium charges for higher grades, not to mention higher charges in general, because the private school kids could afford it . . . all while keeping costs low on our side because we'd only be paying our employees a little extra . . . yep, doable. Mathematically doable.

Physically, I wasn't so sure.

"So we're golden, dude," Camden said with a smile. "Look how many deep pockets are on that list. Kelly's parents are both partners at law firms, Joe Bicher's mom is a plastic surgeon, Dave Malley's got like, old-school foundry money, whatever that means. . . ."

"Yeah, yeah, their bank accounts are golden, and so are we," I said glumly. "As long as my employees and I just don't sleep for the next two weeks." I kept staring at the list of names, already beginning to feel sick to my stomach at the prospect.

"What's more important, sleep or *not* getting us ratted out and expelled?" Camden asked, stopping at a red light.

"Put it that way, why don't you," I muttered.

"It's the truth," he said.

"Yeah, but you don't have to be so blasé about it, especially when you know it's me and my friends who are gonna be writing our butts off, not you," I snapped, my relief at knowing we'd gotten the extra work completely obliterated by the realization that now I'd actually have to *do* the extra work. "If you dealt cocaine, I would totally ask you for some right now," I added. Red Bull was probably not going to cut it any longer.

"Ask me anyway." Camden shrugged. "I can get some."

"Great," I said sarcastically. I looked at the client list again, the rows of names in Camden's blocky handwriting swimming before my eyes, and sighed. Time to buckle down. "So do you have assignments for these people, or what?" I asked.

"Not yet," said Camden. "Which is why we're nowhere near your restaurant right now, if you've noticed." I looked out the window, shaking off my dizziness from having been reading the papers in my lap for the last several minutes. We were actually in his neighborhood, where we stopped in front of a house even bigger than his. There was a tall, curvy blonde in a white tank top and peach yoga pants doing Sun Salutations on the large wraparound porch. She waved as we pulled up.

"Hey, Kel," Camden called through my window at her. "That it?"

Kelly nodded happily, walking around to Camden's side of the car and handing him a backpack, which he passed to me. I noticed the perfect caramel lowlights in her perfect ponytail, and the perfect eyeliner around her perfect big green eyes, and fought my paranoia down again; they dated freshman year, which was ages ago. The only reason they were even talking now was because Camden was saving us. "Kel," Camden said, nodding at me, "this is Maya. Maya, Kelly."

"Nice to meet you." I smiled and gave what I hoped looked like a perky wave.

"Hi!" chirped Kelly, waving back. "I think we might have met at Derek's party a few weeks ago?"

"Oh, right, totally," I said, trying to think back to that night and completely failing to remember; Camden had introduced me to *sooo* many people at Derek's house, a lot of whom had been girls . . . a lot of whom had been hot blond girls. Oh my God. How many of those girls had been girls he'd hooked up with? Great. I felt a sudden urge to take off my seat belt and jump out of the car, and I had to press my back against the seat in order to fight it.

"Thanks, Kel, we're out," Camden said, taking his foot off of the brake. "I'll text you when we're finished on our end." We drove off, Kelly waving over her shoulder as she went back to doing yoga on her porch. I opened the backpack, which was Louis Vuitton, for chrissakes, and started sifting through the assignment sheets from Greenbrook that she had just given us. The problem sets were pretty standard; some of them were even the same as the ones we were already doing for Weston kids, so that was a nice break. I started looking through the book list for English term papers, and all of them seemed pretty standard as well—people needed stuff on *Oliver Twist, Romeo and Juliet, Native Son, Crime and Punishment, Lady Chatterley's Lover* . . .

"Dude, *Lady Chatterley*?" I asked, glancing at Camden. "A little racy, no?"

He shrugged. "Private school." *Lucky them,* I thought. Yet another way the rich kids were having more fun. I continued scanning the contents of Kelly's backpack. The American and European history papers looked like they would be pretty easy to tackle as well, at least in terms of subject matter; most of them were open-ended, "Pick your own thesis and prove it"–type assignments rather than ones with specific questions. Sweet. At any rate, that would make it easier to apply any knowledge we already had. I hate

history but Cat loves it, and Bella and Lucas were experts as
well. I gave Camden a quick kiss as he pulled up around the
corner of the restaurant, then steeled myself for the work
ahead and hopped out of the car. It was time to start farm-
ing these assignments out.

The next week—how shall I put this—blew. I spent what
little free time I had doling out assignments, then collecting them, organizing them—hell, I felt like a teacher—and
then handing them off to Camden. With six full-time
"employees" besides me and a sliding price scale, payroll
now necessitated an Excel spreadsheet; I tried the one my
mom used for the restaurant, and even though I didn't
have to deal with taxes, it was still way more complicated
than I'd ever thought it was going to be. Plus, my emer-
gence from retirement meant that I had to do work on top
of all the organizing—I needed to come up with at least
semi-plausible thesis sentences for papers on books I hadn't
read since sophomore year, and then back them up with
crappy arguments that at least looked like the person was
trying. Hell, I even finally lost my SparkNotes virginity—
I'd never used them before, and the nerd in me felt a little
bad doing it, but I'd done so many shady things in the past
few days (mostly in the form of approaching some of the
junior tutors who seemed cool and clandestinely offering

them money to write some history papers, on the condition that they didn't ask any questions), and the past few weeks, frankly, that throwing another thing onto the pile wasn't any big deal. I was pretty sure that if someone got caught cheating, they didn't get any *more* expelled for cheating with Internet help.

That Friday night, I was alone in the restaurant; my parents and Nat had already gone home, leaving me with the car (awesome) and the responsibility of closing up by myself (not as awesome; with the fine due in only a week, I needed all the free time I could get). It was a warm evening, and I had changed out of my Pailin shirt and back into a gray ribbed tank top. I was clearing the last table in preparation to start vacuuming when I almost dropped a serving dish—at the window, through a crack between the gauzy curtains, Camden's face was doing a blowfish-type move on the glass. He grinned at my momentarily shocked face and came over to the door, drumming his fingers on the metal handle.

"What the hell are you doing here?" I asked as I let him in.

"What? You said you were running the show by yourself tonight." He glanced at my tank top with approval.

"Oh, right," I said. "Ironically, since my parents don't know about the fine, and think I did such a great job while they were away, they're like, a lot more blasé about going home early and leaving me and Nat to deal with closing nowadays." I reached back and turned my ponytail into a loose bun.

"So where's Nat?" Camden asked, looking past me and around the dining room.

"Movie," I answered.

"With Star?" He smirked.

"Of course."

"Well," Camden said, grinning. "How interesting." He stepped forward into the restaurant and bent his head to kiss me. After a moment, I realized something.

"Your mouth was just fully on the outside of that window like, thirty seconds ago." *Ew*.

"Yep, and now whatever was on the glass is on you," he said with a laugh. "Whaddaya got to eat around here?" He made his way behind the bar and started poking around.

"Nothing, kitchen's closed. Well, ice cream. Or drinks." I followed him back there, grabbing a washrag to start wiping down the counter.

"Sweet." Camden grabbed a Singha beer out of the bar fridge.

"Yeah, nice try," I said, taking it out of his hand and putting it back. My mom only counts the bottles every once in a while, but leave it to her to have done it today.

"What about the wine?" Camden asked, pointing to two nearly-empty bottles of red something-or-other that were sitting on the counter by the espresso machine.

I looked at the bottles. "Yeah, go nuts," I said. The handwritten "Opened On" dates on the labels were from last week—we were just going to throw them out anyway.

Camden grinned, grabbed them, and swigged directly from one of the bottles, then the other. "All right. You ready for more assignments?" he asked. "These are all due Monday."

"Lay 'em on me," I said wearily, continuing to tidy up. Camden pulled a list out of his pocket and handed it to me, then hoisted himself onto the counter, swinging his legs back and forth for a moment. "So, what're you doing after this?" He took another swig of wine and looked at me expectantly.

"Finishing closing up here, looking at the list you gave me, taking first dibs on whatever I think is the easiest, and then handing off the rest of the stuff to my friends," I answered mechanically. I threw the washrag I'd been holding into the sink and took my apron off, folding it and putting it in the cabinet by the cash register.

"Wanna come out?" Camden asked. "Dani's thinking bowling, or possibly just driving to bowling and getting drunk in the parking lot."

"Can't. My parents are expecting me home, and even if they weren't, see previous comment about having to write a paper on"—I glanced at the list—"I'm gonna go with *Song of Solomon.*"

"Come on," wheedled Camden. "Work hard, play hard. Right?"

I glared at him.

"Work hard, play flaccid?" he offered, then shrugged. "Well, you gotta do what you gotta do, I guess. And there she is." Camden hopped off the counter and pointed out the front window, where Dani's car, a cute little red-and-white Mini, had just pulled up. She left it running and dashed breathlessly through the front door, wearing a gunmetal gray babydoll dress and open-toed silver heels. What the hell kind of a bowling outfit was that?

"What up, kids?" she said, wrapping her arms easily around Camden's waist for a quick hug. Nothing new there; they were always pretty touchy-feely, but it suddenly bothered me more than it usually did. *Sarah's paranoia strikes again,* I told myself. *Just ignore it or you'll drive yourself crazy.*

"Maya, you coming out?" Dani asked. I shook my head no and she made a pouty face, the expression magnified by the shininess factor of her sheer pink lip gloss. "Dammit!" she said. "Woman, you need to work less. Like, I still can't believe you're not going to the Fling. Thanks for giving this one up, though," she added, poking Camden in the ribs. As if I needed a reminder that the guy I was—dating? hooking up with?—was taking his ex to a dance that my parents wouldn't let me go to.

"Ah, but my after-party . . . my after-party doesn't start until your restaurant shift is over," Camden said, grinning at me. He kissed me good-bye on both the hand and the lips, ignoring Dani's good-natured "Get a room," and the two of them went out the door and got in her car, leaving his parked around the corner. I waved at them and they waved back, peeling away as Camden took out a bottle of Southern Comfort that Dani apparently kept in her glove compartment. He took a swig, then offered it to Dani, who shook her head. How responsible.

Great, I thought to myself, staring out the window as their car disappeared from view. *Just great.* Undoubtedly, they were going to party all weekend, and even though Camden was a champion at texting cute little messages every half hour or so whenever he was out without me— which was a majority of the time, given my evening shifts— it wasn't exactly the most reassuring situation. I mean, I was so busy doing other people's homework that I didn't even have time to hang with my own boyfriend, if I could even call him that. And because of this, I was hypersensitive any time he was hanging out with someone else. Or someone elses. Especially girl versions of the same, and especially sexy, hot, and super-cool ex-girlfriend versions of the same. Hell, *I* thought hanging with Dani was fun, which just made everything worse.

I kept telling myself not to be paranoid, but it was

pointless. Sarah's words echoed in my head as I started walking around the dining room, checking out the table candles to see if any needed to be replaced, and they bumped up against my own thoughts that had been rattling around in my skull from even earlier: A tiger can't change its stripes. Once a player, always a player. Who in school *hadn't* Camden already hooked up with? I had a feeling the list was short indeed . . . mostly because, if I bothered to think about any of the stories I'd heard about him since sophomore year, I could start listing off the girls myself. Dani and Stacey, both of whom he was still friends with. Lara O'Connor. Hayden Ford. Aubrey Stern. Allison Scaney-Gray. All four Kolardie sisters. (Okay, that one was *probably* a rumor. As far as anybody knew, he'd only dated one of them, but they all looked weirdly the same despite their different ages, and they liked to joke about switching places.) Still, it made my stomach hurt just thinking about it, and when I saw the list of assignments from Greenbrook that Camden had brought over, and remembered that I wouldn't be going to sleep for at least another six hours, my head started hurting too.

Ugh.

I looked at the bar, where the bottles that Camden had been drinking out of were still sitting, and matter-of-factly drained them both into my mouth before tossing them in the recycle bin. It would have been more dramatic if there'd been more than a teaspoon of wine left in either of them, but I figured it was the gesture that counted.

Saturday morning, when I got a text from Bella's friend Darren asking me to call either him or Lucas, I figured they just had a routine question about payment dates or their next assignment. Of course, bad things seemed to be happening to me lately, not so much in threes as in three hundreds.

"Darren, what's up?" I said into my phone when he answered. I'd ducked outside the restaurant during a lull in the lunch shift, and was huddled near the mailboxes, trying to stay out of yet another round of spring drizzle. At least nowadays it was usually warm spring drizzle.

"Hey, Maya," said Darren. "Look, Lucas and I don't think we're gonna be able to finish our papers this weekend. Can you get someone else do to them?"

"Oh," I said, feeling my neck tense up and my stomach drop to my feet.

"Yeah, I mean, thanks for the extra work and all. We love the money—"

"We do," chimed in a voice from the background; Lucas was apparently there with him. "But it's kind of too much to do right now, especially since the S.A.T.s are coming up and we're both taking a Kaplan course."

"No problem," I said, struggling to remain upright; I'd

never fainted before, but I was pretty sure this is what the moment before passing out felt like. "Thanks for letting me know." I hung up, then mentally screamed, "*Aaaaaah-hhhhh!*" before flinging myself dramatically against the mailboxes, which made a muffled clanging sound. Cat had already e-mailed to tell me that Bella was begging off because of the extra off-season workouts her volleyball coach had just instituted, and now these guys? There was no point in arguing, though, or trying to convince them otherwise—who could blame them, really? Everyone already had their own work to do, especially as it was getting to be so late in the semester, and it wasn't like anybody besides me needed, or even wanted, to make more than a few hundred bucks a week, tops. I couldn't stop people from flaking. I just had to pick up the slack.

Me.

Myself.

I.

Yeah, there was no way that was going to happen.

"We're totally screwed," I whispered to Camden on the phone late that night, after work. I was under the covers of my bed; my parents were asleep, but there was no point in taking chances.

"We're not," he said. "I'll write some of the goddamn papers if we have to, but we're not screwed."

I literally dropped the phone in surprise, although

since I was lying down, it only had about two inches to fall. I picked it back up. "You'll what?"

"I'll write some. They'll be bad," he warned. "But if we need to, I can do it."

"Oh my God. That's so sweet of you," I said, my voice squeaking through the whisper.

"Or," he said, "we could go with my original plan and kick Leonard's ass."

"Yeah, right. Man, I wish there was some other way. . . ." I used the glow from my phone to go over the assignment lists for Greenbrook and Weston again, wondering where the hell I might be able to cut corners. And then it hit me.

Everywhere.

As long as nobody from Weston ever talked to anybody from Greenbrook . . . there was a good fifty percent overlap between assignments, especially on the history papers where people could pick their own topics.

"Camden?" I whispered, hardly able to breathe; I was at once ecstatic and terrified, and I wriggled my head out from under the blankets in order to get more air. "What do you think the odds are of us getting caught if we start selling the same papers to the Weston kids and the Greenbrook kids?"

There was a long pause. "Well," he said carefully, "a lot higher than they were before, for sure."

"So you don't think we should do it?" I asked.

"Please," he said. "I'm bummed we didn't start doing it earlier." But his voice didn't have its usual bravado.

Neither of us said anything for a while.

"You're worried, aren't you?" I said finally.

"Actually, yeah," Camden answered.

We both knew we had to do it anyway.

I wish I could say that our grand decision to sell duplicate papers cut my work in half. Well, actually it sort of did, almost. We were able to double up on just over a third of the assignments, once all was said and done. But "horrifying train wreck" divided by two is still half a horrifying train wreck, especially when it is preceded by several weeks of preliminary train wreckage. I skipped a few classes for the first time ever, figuring that I could always get notes from someone else, whereas I needed this money now. Besides, Stanford wouldn't care if I had a few unexcused absences on my attendance record (I assumed), but I was pretty sure they'd care if I got expelled for cheating. I didn't know what scared me more at this point—missing out on Stanford if Leonard ratted me out for cheating, or missing out on Stanford if my parents found out about the fine and shipped me off to Thailand. The prospect of either kept me motivated to churn out the papers, even though the circles under my eyes were threatening to invade the rest of my face, while the blood churning through my veins was probably about eighty percent Mountain Dew.

My daily schedule that week, from the end of school until work, and then again from the end of work until I passed out for a few short hours, went a little something like this: typing, typing, reading, vision blurring, typing, typing, wrists cramping, fingers gnarling, falling asleep on the keyboard, lather, rinse, caffeine, typing, repeat. Jonny, trying to help, gave me this funky voice recognition software that he downloaded illegally, but after I started off somebody's paper by dictating "While 'The Snows of Kilimanjaro' would have been effective even without Harry's memories," and it ended up on-screen as "White shows kill a manger flex evening with a hairy man or ease," I gave up on that. Jonny, Cat, and the others had their own methods for dealing with the hellish work, but we were all too busy to even commiserate with one another, except for the occasional bitchy text message. It sucked. Everything sucked.

But Camden saved me. Any time I started feeling so exhausted that I wanted to cut corners, he would either talk me out of it or pick up the slack. When I forgot to highlight the assignments with obscene pictures to force our clients to copy them into their own writing before turning them in—still a serious security compromise—Camden would make sure to do it. His favorite method was to write, *Please tell the guidance counselor that I am contemplating teen suicide and this is a cry for help,* and his second favorite was the phrase *I have syphilis.* When I didn't have time to print out papers and give him hard copies, he told me to start e-mailing them to him so that he could do it himself, and—once again thinking of security—created new fake e-mail accounts for both of us just for this purpose. Even when I was two seconds from passing out for the night after having written yet another C-level paper on why "Madame Bovary was *so* justified in being a big ho," I had to giggle when I logged in as tinyhotasian@gmail.com and sent files to midwesternstud@gmail.com.

It sucked, and it sucked, and I didn't sleep, and I didn't sleep some more, and then, suddenly or finally, I couldn't tell which, F-day arrived. F-day being, of course, the absolute last day to pay off the Health Department fine before the penalties started kicking in. I owed Leonard, too, but I was taking care of that tomorrow. (Technically I'd owed him a few days ago, but I'd managed to convince him to give me an extension by standing really, really close to him and whispering my request directly in his ear. It was the closest to prostitution that I'd ever come.) The important part was, I now had the money for both payoffs—$15,000 in cash (and a little extra, actually, that I was planning on using to buy myself a little something extremely frivolous and to-be-determined) hidden in various places around my room. Camden had been good about making sure to pay me in crisp new hundreds, so at least the money didn't take up that much physical space; most of it was tucked between my mattress and box spring—a cliché but effective hiding place—and the rest was in random spots around my closet.

That Friday morning, I put together two fat envelopes of cash and stuck the Health Department one between some books in my backpack, praying that I would make it through the school day and then to the Health Department without getting robbed, or into an accident, or waylaid by a plague of locusts, or distracted by the sudden appearance of Christian Bale declaring his love for me. I then used a clip to pull my hair out of my face and dressed in an outfit—black pants, a pale blue sleeveless shell, a black cardigan sweater, and black heels—that I thought would hopefully make me look at least marginally older and therefore less suspicious when I walked into the Health Department. I checked myself out in the mirror. Okay, now instead of seventeen I looked . . . like a college sophomore going to a summer job interview. Well, better than nothing. I threw my rarely used fake Coach purse into my backpack as a finishing touch on my "disguise" and prepared to take off for the Health Department the second the sixth-period bell rang.

"You look like my mom," Camden said. He was already in the car by the time I got there after school, and he looked at my outfit with a mixture of amusement and barely disguised revulsion as he turned the key in the ignition.

"Guess we shouldn't make out then," I said dryly. He was right, though—I'd added a strand of fake pearls that I'd dug out of my fourth-grade dress-up box to my official fine-paying outfit at the last minute, resulting in a vaguely sad "Dress for the job you want, not the job you have" sort of look. I buckled my seat belt as Camden peeled out of the parking lot and headed downtown, then took the fake Coach out of my backpack and threw the envelope of cash into it. Of course, when we got there, Camden dropped me off at the door of the building and then decided to circle the block in lieu of waiting in the adjoining parking structure, and I forgot that I had put the cash into the purse and ended up carrying both my backpack and the purse into the Health Department. This meant that as I walked in, I had to ditch my backpack by the door and kick it under a crappy end table in a way that I hoped was subtle, but probably wasn't. Whatever, I was here. Finally.

I walked up to the drab gray counter. In terms of its general atmosphere, the Health Department was pretty much a facsimile of the D.M.V., though with a lot fewer

people waiting around. So far, so good. The only thing standing between me and freedom was the disheveled, fortyish
woman manning the window, whose nametag said MANDY
and whose overall demeanor said, "Is it the weekend yet?"

"Hi," I said to Mandy. "I'm here to pay off the fine for
Pailin Thai Restaurant."

Mandy looked at me skeptically. "Usually that's done
by mail. Do you have the citation number?"

"Uh, yeah . . ." I fumbled through my purse for the
original letter from Richard (or, as I had been calling him
for the past month and a half, Dick) R. Jenkins. "Here it is,"
I said, handing her the now fairly crumpled paper.

She glanced at it. "And will you be paying by check or
credit card?"

"Cash."

Mandy raised an eyebrow at me. I smiled sweetly.

"Okay," she said warily, and handed me a form to fill
out. "I'll need to see some ID." I put the envelope of cash and
my driver's license onto the counter, trying to look casual.
Mandy opened it, her eyes widening a little, and then took
a very, very long time counting everything out. A line began
to build up behind me. I hoped everyone was as bored as
they looked and not paying attention to what was going on,
as Mandy had to call a supervisor in to back up her own
counting by recounting, as well as to mark every single bill
with one of those anti-counterfeit pens.

"You're all set," she finally said, after what seemed like forever but was actually just long enough for blisters to start forming on both of my feet from standing there in my heels and shifting my weight around nervously.

"Thank you!" I said, gratefully taking the receipt she handed me. "So we're clear? We won't be getting any more notices in the mail?"

"You shouldn't. At least, not until you flunk another inspection," she said. *Ouch.*

My heart still felt about a million pounds lighter.

I went outside, and Camden pulled up to where I was waiting on the sidewalk. I got back into his car with a literal spring in my step. I kicked off my heels, yanked off the cardigan and the fake pearls, took my hair down, let it fall over my shoulders and into my face, and breathed a sigh of relief.

"One down," Camden said, leaning over and pressing his forehead to mine.

"One to go," I answered.

I floated through that evening's restaurant shift, trembling with the happy knowledge that the nightmare of the fine was behind me, but keenly aware that I still had the Leonard issue to deal with the next morning. Would he ask for more money? Would I have to keep the cheating ring going? I didn't want to think about it; I was looking forward to my first full night's sleep in almost a month.

Of course, when you're that sleep-deprived, even ten hours feels like two, and Leonard was already sitting at a corner table, engrossed in a copy of *Entertainment Weekly*, when I rushed into the downtown Starbucks where he'd told me to meet him. I was armed with the other envelope of cash that I'd prepared yesterday, and oh-so-ready to put the rest of the nightmarish last few weeks behind me. I only hoped that he wasn't planning on pulling some incredibly obnoxious last-minute move, like charging me interest for being twenty minutes late.

"Hey there, you finally made it," Leonard said, waving me over with a big grin. "Sit down. You want anything? On me. This thing is apparently a peppermint Frap." He indicated the rather girly-looking drink on the table in front of him.

"I just want to get out of here A.S.A.P.," I said icily, and watched as his face fell for a moment before turning back into a now fake-looking grin. "Here." I shoved the cash at him without bothering to sit down. He started to open the envelope. "Oh my God, seriously?" I asked. "You're gonna count it *here*? It's not like you don't know where to find me if I screwed it up somehow."

"Of course I'm counting it here," Leonard said pleasantly, making a big show of rolling up his sleeves. "I mean, you're a cheater. You obviously can't be trusted, and I already gave you a few extra days. Why don't you just calm down?"

I resisted the urge to snap his reedy little neck and instead sighed deeply and plunked myself down in the chair across from him. He opened the envelope and started counting the bills; to his credit, he did it by sticking his hands inside the envelope and keeping them there, so that no one could tell what was inside if they didn't bother to really look . . . which the coffee-downing, noisily chattering morning crowd around us wasn't bothering to do.

"Did you know that Derek Rowe's sister got a boob job?" he asked conversationally as he counted.

"No," I said coldly, while silently filing that information away in my head to tell Cat later. No wonder Bella said that Abby Rowe had missed an entire week of volleyball practice toward the end of the season. Probably didn't want to be jumping around with all the extra new weight. Or, God forbid, having to dive for a bump. "Are you done yet?" I asked.

"I am," Leonard said, closing the envelope and tucking in the flap. "It's all here, thanks. This'll work for now." He got up, throwing a twenty on the table. "I gotta go, but if you want, get yourself a cappuccino or something. It's on me."

"You already said that, and I already ignored you," I said, shoving his money back at him. "And what do you mean by 'this works for now'? I'm done. I'm retired. I'm not doing this anymore."

"You might have to," said Leonard. He was smiling, but there was an ominous hint in his voice. "Don't worry, though. I'll give you plenty of advance notice." I stared at him in disbelief as he walked off, literally whistling a jaunty tune. He couldn't—he wasn't going to—screw that! I was graduating in two months. If he thought he was going to have time to blackmail me any further, he was mistaken. Well, actually he wasn't mistaken, since he had two months to blackmail me further, but for now . . .

For now, it was over.

Oh my God. I closed my eyes and breathed deeply. Okay. It was over. I was so angry at Leonard's last-minute threat that I wanted to throw a chair at his skinny little back as it disappeared out the door, but—it was over.

Oh my God, it was over!

A spontaneous grin broke out on my face, and it grew even wider when I heard my phone chime and I opened it to find a text from Camden: *Everything go ok?*

I called him. "Everything indeed went okay," I said happily, leaning back and kicking my feet up on the chair that Leonard had just vacated. I looked around at the crowd of cheerful Starbucks faces, and even the few grumpy ones, and knew that I had just seamlessly transitioned from being one of the latter to one of the former. "I mean," I continued, "he sort of threatened that he might—but you know what, don't even worry about it. Everything went okay."

"Awesome," Camden said. "Uh, so . . . what time do you think you're gonna be over here later?" Spring Fling was that evening, and even though I would be stuck at work while Camden was getting his dance on with Dani and the rest of his pals, I was still supposed to head over to the after-party he was throwing at his house. It was probably going to go all night—his parents were out of town again, as usual.

"I don't know," I said, wondering why he sounded a little tense before chalking it up to my own recently alleviated paranoia of the past few weeks. "Depends on how crowded the restaurant is tonight. Probably some time after eleven. Maybe closer to midnight?" I checked my watch and started to get up; speaking of the restaurant, it was almost time for my lunch shift.

"Well, you know where I'll be," Camden said.

"Facedown on the floor drunk?" I asked.

"Actually, I'll probably drink in the hot tub. Quicker that way."

"Try to stay conscious until I get there."

"Don't worry. I'll save you a spot."

I giggled. We said good-bye and hung up, and I fairly skipped to the bus stop to head to work. The lunch shift ended up being brutal, and the dinner shift was our most crowded night in weeks, but I somehow managed to juggle everything perfectly—no missed orders, no mistakes, nothing but a smile for every single customer. My parents and Nat all commented at one point or another on my great mood and the sunshine radiating from my voice; I just smiled mysteriously and asked, "What, can't a girl be happy every once in a while for no reason?"

"No" was Nat's answer.

"You are my favorite little brother!" I squealed at him; I reached up and ruffled his hair, all the while balancing an entire tray full of lime sodas. He looked at me strangely as I giggled like an idiot, practically drunk from my good mood. I hadn't thought it was possible to be any happier than I was a few weeks ago, when I'd gotten that letter from Stanford, but that had lasted only a few minutes before Leonard ruined it, whereas my present giddiness had been steadily growing for hours now.

The delirium from being so tired for so many days in a row certainly wasn't helping to calm me down, and neither were the four Thai iced coffees I drank during the dinner shift, so when Cat and I got to Camden's house later that night, I practically ran down the stairs ahead of her to the basement, low-fiving people on the way like a huge dork, hollering, "Hey!" at anyone who glanced in my direction, even downing a shot that someone handed to me on the fly. At the basement door, I squeezed in between Stacey and

Nate, who were both examining the fake henna tattoo she'd just put around her belly button.

"Nice, Maya!" Nate hooted as I rushed past them, peeling off my T-shirt to reveal the top of that cute little red bikini I'd bought a few weeks back, in preparation for hopping into the hot tub with Camden. I should have felt self-conscious—there were a few other girls in bikinis, but most of the people were still in their Spring Fling dresses or suits, albeit in various states of disarray—but by that point I was in too good of a mood. I grinned at Nate and did a little mock shimmy at him, eliciting an appreciative whistle, and then turned back to the hot tub. I got two steps closer before I realized what was going on in it.

Camden and Dani were making out.

I stopped dead in my tracks, my eyes widening, my heart pounding, my breath catching and sticking in my throat. They say when you're about to die, your entire life flashes before your eyes. Well, now I know that when you're about to kill someone, the same thing happens. Except that instead of your entire life, it's just the moments you had spent with that person, and as every moment flashes by, it now contains a chain saw.

"You *asshole*!" I screamed, so loudly that everyone in the room could hear me over the music. They all turned to stare as I took a few steps closer to the hot tub, staring daggers at Camden and Dani the whole way, and just barely resisting picking up a beer can off the floor and throwing it. "I can't believe I ever trusted you!"

Camden calmly disengaged himself from Dani's lips, just long enough to turn in my direction and smirk. "Yeah, I can't believe you ever did either," he said.

The room was silent. I stood there for a moment, silent as well. Furious. Devastated. Wanting to kill. Wanting to die.

Then I turned around, not caring that everyone could see that I was crying, and walked out.

chapter seventeen

I spent the rest of the weekend mentally beating myself to a pulp. How had I, a smart girl with a good, practical head on her shoulders (if I did say so myself), fallen for the biggest man-whore in school? How had I let him use and humiliate me like that? Had he and Dani been hooking up the whole time? Had everyone known and been laughing at me for weeks? Worst of all, did I deserve the pain? Was it my own fault for being such a colossal idiot? *Yeah*, I answered myself. *Yeah, I do deserve it.* I was just as stupid as every other girl in the history of time who thought that a sketchpad had finally changed because of her. Lesson learned. Lesson brutally, mortifyingly learned.

Of course, that didn't stop me from spending all of Sunday obsessively checking my cell and e-mail every two minutes, in case Camden called or texted or wrote. I wasn't planning on picking up or texting him back—while

I desperately missed what had become an almost constant electronic stream of snarky flirtiness, or flirty snarkiness, I wanted the satisfaction of *not* doing any of that—but he never did send any communication, so the satisfaction never came. The only calls I got were from Cat, which I let go to voice mail; the only texts I got were from Jonny, none of which I bothered to read—they probably wanted to console me about Camden, but I didn't want to talk to anyone, including them. Basically, any time on Sunday that I wasn't working at the restaurant, I was holed up in my room, calling through the door whenever someone knocked to say that I was fine, just doing a lot of homework, when the reality was that I was crying into a pillow, and occasionally yelling into it—at myself. At one point, when all my tears seemed to have run out, I tried catching up on all my own homework that I'd been ignoring lately; the attempt lasted about fourteen seconds before my body found some sort of hydration reserve and I started crying all over again. And when I *was* at work, I had such a fake smile of complete happiness pasted on my face that I single-handedly brought our tips to forty percent above the average for a Sunday. Wow. I should've dated sketchpads and had them cheat on me the entire past month or so—I could've paid off the fine without having to do anything illegal.

But then Monday morning came, and I couldn't hide anymore. I listened to Beyoncé's "Irreplaceable" several times as I was getting ready, mostly because "I Will Survive" seemed a little too middle-aged divorcée, and carefully chose an outfit—my lowest-rise jeans, a dark gray fitted sweater with a deep V-neck, and chunky black shoes that made me two inches taller—that I hoped walked the line between "I look so freakin' hot, it doesn't matter that I got publicly cheated on two days ago" and "I don't care about same."

By the time I arrived at school, I had pasted on my fake cheerful smile from the weekend, but it quickly disappeared as I heard the murmurs in the hallway, from "Dude, did you hear?" to "Yeah, Camden and Dani . . ." to "Brutal, just brutal, man." My smile failing, I aimed for an expression that I hoped looked convincingly neutral, and for a moment, I thought it was working.

And then Cat and Jonny approached my locker.

"Hi," they said, their faces grim and their voices hard. Around us, everyone was in a rush to get to first period, because the bell was about to ring, but when I shut my locker door and turned to look at them, Cat and Jonny were both standing stock-still.

"Hey," I said hesitantly, not really sure what those oddly focused looks on their faces meant; Cat was standing with her arms crossed, and Jonny's hand was poised at an odd angle on his backpack strap. They both stared at me. "Sorry I didn't answer your calls yesterday," I started. "I was—"

"Save it," Cat snapped.

I involuntarily took a tiny step back. "What?"

"She said save it," Jonny said. "We *know*."

My heart, already living somewhere in the soles of my feet for the past day and a half, sank even lower. The rest of me wanted to follow it; if I could have melted into the floor at that exact moment and disappeared from the planet, I would have.

"We know about the money," Jonny continued, looking a tiny bit satisfied as my face went white. "We know you were skimming. We heard about it at the party, after you left."

I opened my mouth, then closed it again, then opened it again. "How did you—"

"People start talking when they get drunk," Cat said flatly. "And there we were, feeling *sooo* bad that you just got cheated on, when you were cheating *us* the whole time."

Oh my God.

I backed up some more, so that my entire body was pressed against my locker; I was pretty sure that I needed the support to remain standing. "I'm sorry," I stammered, feeling somewhat like a deer in headlights but more like a deer that had already been thoroughly smashed all over the road by an SUV. "I'm so, so sorry . . . it's just that—I mean, I—you don't understand—"

"And we don't want to," Cat said, her voice as cold as

ice. "You're damn right you're sorry, because you should
be." She and Jonny both stared daggers at me, then turned
around and walked away.

The bell rang.

I didn't move. I'd thought that seeing Camden and
Dani making out in his basement was the lowest point in
my life so far, but now I knew that there was lower. Way
lower.

After a long moment, I felt a pair of eyes on me, and I
looked up to realize that Sarah was standing in the hallway,
only a few feet away, staring. She'd heard everything.

"Sarah . . ." I said hesitantly.

She walked away from me too.

Ten minutes later, when I'd finally gathered the strength to
start trudging down the hallway toward history—detention
slip in hand; a hall monitor had spotted me and wasn't
taking "Uh, my world just collapsed?" as an excuse—I was
never more glad that Camden and I didn't have any classes
together, and never more sorry that Jonny, Cat, Sarah, and
I did. It took most of my strength to keep from skipping
the entire school day and hiding out in the bathroom until
it was time to go to work, and the rest of it to keep from
breaking down crying in class as I walked in and took my
seat—inevitably one near Cat, or Jonny, or Sarah, or all

three. I sat silently as they all ignored me and cheerfully, pointedly talked to one another; if it's possible to radiate waves of icy hatred toward a person by simply smiling at someone else, that's what they were all doing to me. It took me until fourth period to steel myself enough that I was able to plunk into my seat without having to blink back tears. I was resigned to making it through the rest of the year, and graduation, and the summer, without any friends, and I opened up my notebook in preparation to pay the closest attention in class that I had in weeks.

Although clearly I wasn't paying attention *that* well, because a few minutes after Mr. Traynor started talking, I saw Camden walk by in the hallway, and that wouldn't have happened unless I'd been staring out the classroom door window. He was skipping class as usual, I guessed, and I immediately had a horrible flashback to the hot-tub scene from Saturday night, while simultaneously picturing him dramatically throwing Dani down onto a Chem lab table and ripping off whatever tiny scrap of an excuse for a shirt she happened to be wearing. But a split second later I saw Principal Davis following him, and then Vice Principal Rooker. They all looked grim, and they were all heading toward the administrative wing.

Oh God. That couldn't be good.

I fidgeted my way through the rest of the hour, then walked by Camden's Government class before fifth period to see if he was there. He wasn't, although maybe he was going to show up late, which wouldn't be a surprise. Sixth period, I asked for a hall pass and swung by his English class for a casual peek in the window. He wasn't there either. And after school, when I went out to the parking lot to check and see if his car was there, I could see that it wasn't.

Something had happened. Something had definitely happened. Had he been busted for the cheating ring? Was that why he'd been yanked out of class by Principal Davis? Hell, if my friends had figured out what was going on, it wouldn't be too surprising if the school had too. Was I just minutes away from going down in flames as well? Oh God, it was over. It was so over. Good-bye, Stanford. Hello, Thailand. My parents were going to ship me overseas so fast, I wouldn't have time to kick myself any more than I'd already been doing. Of course, it didn't matter anymore; all my friends had abandoned me anyway, and with good reason.

I nervously dug my fingernails into my own palms, realized it hurt, and kept doing it anyway as I spun away from the parking lot and walked toward the bus stop to catch my first non-Camden ride to work in weeks. It was a sunny day, but I didn't bother to put on my shades—I wanted the torture of the too-bright sky in my eyes. Was it possible that Camden had been busted for something else? I mean, he'd been dragged away to the principal's office hours ago, and if it had been about the cheating ring, they would've certainly gotten to me by the end of the day. It had to be something else, right? Maybe there was some other business he had going on the side that I'd never known about . . . drugs, or gambling, or hookers? Okay, probably not hookers. Either way, he was a jerk. If he went down in flames, but somehow I got off scot-free, that was fine. That would be the universe giving me a teeny-tiny reward. All my friends already hated me, so there was no reason for me to have to get expelled and make my own life even worse. If I were found out, I would surely lose my Stanford acceptance, and now literally the *only* thing I had going for me was the prospect of getting the hell out of this town in August. Granted, I'd be going there having lost my best friend, but hey, starting over is what college is for. It didn't matter that I had nothing left here. I'd just leave. Forget everything. Start again. Right?

The bus pulled up to the bus stop and I stepped onto it and settled into a seat. I clutched my backpack on my lap and stared out the window in the direction of the school, blinking back tears.

Suddenly, I knew I wouldn't be able to live with myself if I didn't do anything.

And then, I knew exactly what I had to do.

chapter eighteen

"Mom? Dad? Can I talk to you for a second?" It was four thirty and I had just gotten to the restaurant, after deliberately getting off the bus a few stops early in order to walk for a while and clear my head. My parents were up from their between-shifts naps and were getting ready for dinner; Nat was at Science Olympiad practice and would probably be late. For once I was glad, instead of bitter, that I had to hold down the first hour of our shift solo—he didn't need to witness what was about to go down, especially since afterward he was going to be an only child.

"It's really serious," I added, because my mom had merely nodded in my direction and then continued to putter around the dining room, putting out little standing ads for our new dessert—a lychee sorbet that my dad had recently perfected—on every table. She looked up at me and saw that I wasn't kidding, and yelled toward the kitchen for my dad to come out. He did so, carrying a mortar and pestle filled with peanuts that he was crushing by hand, and they both sat down at one of the tables. My mom tucked her hair behind her ears, clasped her hands together, and visibly steeled herself.

"Did Nat get a girl pregnant?" she asked.

"What? No! I don't think so," I said, a little skeeved out. "Wow, you led with that instead of asking me if *I'm* pregnant?"

"You are more responsible than Nat," shrugged my dad good-naturedly, taking his baseball hat off and setting it on the table. "Besides, you can't be pregnant. Can you?" He shot a nervous sidelong glance at me.

"No, I can't," I said. "And gross. It's nothing like that."

My dad visibly relaxed. "Okay, then what is it? You said serious." My parents looked at me expectantly, Mom now absently polishing a fork with a corner of the little silk scarf she was wearing, Dad still crushing the peanuts. I started to sit down across from them and then thought better of it—I didn't want to be within arm's length of my mom and her fork once I got done talking. "Uh . . . remember when you guys went to Auntie Jintana's wedding a while back?" I asked.

They looked at each other. "I told you she was too young to run the restaurant," my mom said accusingly. "See? Something went wrong."

"Just let her say whatever it is she's going to say," my

dad snapped back at her. Great, they were already mad. I debated giving the panicky, "You've gotta help me" version of the story I'd told Camden a few weeks ago, or the "It wasn't really my fault, so please feel sorry for me" version I'd given Sarah more recently. Then I thought about my friends, whom I'd horribly betrayed, and about Camden, trudging his way to the principal's office, and I opted for the just plain truth.

And so, once again came the story, as simply as I could tell it: the chaos that weekend they went away. The two psycho bitch customers. Nat and me being zonked and skimping on the cleanup. The health inspector, the $10,000 fine—here, my mom took such a deep, sudden breath that I thought all the silverware on the table would be sucked into her lungs. My dad wordlessly held up a hand for me to stop talking, got up, took the top off of a Singha beer and handed it to my mom, got one for himself as well, sat back down, and gestured for me to continue. I did. I told them how afraid I was that they'd exact some sort of terrible punishment on me, how I didn't want them or Nat to worry, how I didn't want us to lose the restaurant. I told them about Camden's offer to pay me for homework, and how we took that idea and built it into a business that eventually paid the fine, and Leonard's blackmail. I told them that our cheating ring had been discovered and that Camden had probably gotten expelled, but that he didn't appear to have taken me down with him . . . not yet, at any rate. I told them that I didn't want to lie to them anymore, so I was telling them the truth, and that I was planning on coming clean at school, too. I deliberately left out all the personal stuff about me and Camden—it wasn't technically relevant, and there was no point in getting them even more worried than they already were.

By now, my dad was on his second beer, although my mom hadn't touched hers. "Why didn't you tell your brother?" Mom asked. "He was there that weekend too."

"You put me in charge," I said. "It was my responsibility, not his. I didn't want to worry him, either."

As Mom and Dad exchanged a glance that I couldn't read, we all heard a knock—a customer was at the door, where none of us had bothered to flip the lock or change the CLOSED sign to OPEN yet, even though it was now past five. My parents both ignored the guy. I shot him an apologetic look through the window and shrugged, and he suddenly looked very uncomfortable and turned away. It was only then that I realized that I was crying. Well, not quite sobbing or anything, but my cheeks were streaked with tears that I didn't remember falling.

"I'm sorry!" I said to my parents. "I'm so sorry! It's all my fault. I let you down."

"Why didn't you just tell us when we came back?" asked Dad.

"Because I was scared!" I wailed. "And I didn't want you to worry about it! It was all my fault, and—"

"Yes, it was," my mom said.

"I know, and—"

"No," my dad said. "Be quiet. Now we get to talk."

I shut up. "Can I get one of those beers?" I asked, taking a lame stab at lightening the mood. To my dad's credit, he actually hesitated before saying no. Then, he and my mom launched into a very long lecture that: a) I fully deserved, b) I knew was coming, c) I had just asked for, and d) was horrible to listen to anyway. They pointed out that what started as a small, routine problem with unruly customers had turned into a bigger one when we got lazy with the cleaning, which then turned into a bigger one when the health inspector showed up, which completely spiraled out of control when I decided to fix my original mistake with an elaborate one. They explained that this was why they were so strict all the time; they didn't think they could always trust my judgment; they took a gamble that weekend and thought it paid off, but clearly it hadn't. Then they hit me up with that tried-and-true parental classic—they weren't angry, they were disappointed. "Well, okay, also a little angry," my dad said, his chin on his hand, his mortar and pestle shoved to the side and forgotten. "But mostly disappointed."

I looked at my dad, then at my mom, then back at my dad, then back at my mom . . . and then I started sobbing in relief. My mom came over to my side of the table and hugged me as I unfolded all four of the napkins I had carefully folded yesterday and shoved them into my face.

"Next time, tell the truth," Mom said gently.

"I know," I cried into the napkins.

"And you have to go to school and tell them, too," my dad added.

"I know," I sniffled, looking up slightly. "I'm sorry. I just knew we couldn't have paid the fine—"

"Yes, we could have," said my mom. "Let your dad and me worry about things like that."

"No, we couldn't, I knew we couldn't. I saw it on the spreadsheet—it was all red numbers, and now if I tell the school I cheated, they're gonna call the scholarship people and then we *really* won't be able to afford Stanford. . . . We can't afford anything. . . . I'm going to be stuck here forever. . . . I'm so sorry. . . ." I started crying all over again.

"What are you talking—?" my mom started.

"The computer. I saw the computer, with the Excel files for the restaurant. We don't have any money. . . ."

My mom sighed. "You think the restaurant is doing badly? You think we could have run this place for twenty years if we were losing money on it?" As if to underscore her point, a group of six people approached the door, and one of them yanked on the handle, only to find that it was still locked. They looked at us, confused, through the window. My dad waved them off.

"I don't know," I said. "No, I guess. But—"

"But nothing. We are not rich, but we have enough. And there is an extra bank account for your college tuition and for Nat's."

I looked up. "What?"

"We have been saving for you two all of your lives. We can pay for school. Maybe not the most expensive school, but with financial aid, we will be able to make it work."

"You will be paying off your loans for a long time, of course," my dad said.

"Wait, what? There's an extra bank account?" I asked; my hands clutched two of the tearstained napkins frantically. "I thought the tip jar was the only . . ." I trailed off, totally bewildered, and looked from my mom to my dad and back again.

My parents sighed. "You don't know everything," Mom said. "You just think you do, like every other teenager." She got up and unlocked the front door, flipping the sign to OPEN. The conversation was pretty much over, I guessed. It was a relief to get everything out in the open, and an even bigger relief to know that my family wasn't two inches away from bankruptcy and starvation, but . . . I thought of something.

"Mom? Dad? Once I tell the school what I did, they're gonna have to tell Stanford. Do you think they'll revoke my acceptance?"

None of us knew the answer.

chapter nineteen

The next morning, I skipped first period and went straight to Principal Davis's office. I figured that I should get a jump on the day, and on my expulsion, because, assuming it was going to happen, there was no point in going to class. Instead, I was planning on confessing that I'd been running the whole operation with Camden, while making sure that I didn't incriminate anyone else, and then watching myself go merrily down in flames like I darn well deserved to. The last thing I did before trudging down to the administrative wing was to leave an apology note in Sarah's locker; she wasn't speaking to me, just like everyone else, and I didn't expect her forgiveness, but I felt like she should at least know what I was planning to do.

Of course, it didn't look like I was going to be able to do it as quickly as I thought—when I got to the principal's office, three kids were already lined up ahead of me: Trent

Zeeb, who had undoubtedly set yet another thing on fire, which he's been doing since the first grade (he's never hurt anybody, actually, just singed and melted a bunch of stuff); Candace Rilker, who probably wasn't in trouble but was just there to register yet another formal complaint about the lack of condom machines in the bathrooms; and some guy I didn't know, but whose age and number of tattoos clearly both outnumbered twenty. I sat down in the chair next to him and found myself engaged in a rousing bout of mind over matter in order to avoid gagging, since apparently he hadn't showered in a while.

It took until third period for my turn to come up; by then, figuring that schoolwork was pointless, I had read and reread all the texts on my phone, and methodically erased all the ones sent to and from Camden. He *had* gotten expelled, that I knew for sure now; I'd heard the chatter in the hallways as soon as I'd stepped inside the school that morning. I wondered what effect my looming confession was going to have on Principal Davis—maybe, I thought hopefully, once he found out that there had been two of us behind the scheme instead of just one, he'd dilute our punishment. Maybe he'd revoke Camden's expulsion and slap us both with suspensions instead.

But he would probably just expel me, too.

An incoming IM noise beeped on Mrs. Hunter's

computer. "Maya?" she said, looking up from her monitor. "Thank you for waiting. You can go right in."

Well, I was about to find out.

I took a deep breath, picked up my backpack, and pushed open the heavy wooden door to Principal Davis's office. It swung shut behind me with a thud, and I jumped a little at the sound.

"Maya!" Principal Davis roared. "Come in! Sorry about that door. Sit down!"

I sat down.

"What can I do you for, young lady?"

In the giant chair across from his desk, my feet didn't even touch the ground. I swung them nervously as Principal Davis picked up his stapler and fiddled with it for a minute. When he finally stopped and looked up at me, I sat forward in the chair and blurted out, "You know how you expelled Camden King yesterday for cheating?"

"Yes," he said. The pleasant look on his face was gone, replaced by one I couldn't read. "Why is this any concern of yours?"

"Because-I-helped-him," I said quickly.

"What?"

"I helped him," I repeated, slower this time. I wasn't nervous anymore. I was walking the plank, and for some reason, I suddenly had a desire to do it gracefully.

Principal Davis put down his stapler and leaned

forward in his chair. "Maya," he said quietly, "you're a very smart girl. And I know that you've been spending time with Camden and my daughter and their other friends lately. But that's no reason for you to lie to try to help him. You've got a bright future."

"I'm not lying," I said. "I'm telling the truth. And I'm not doing it to help him. I'm doing it because it's the right thing to do." Did I want to help a disgusting two-faced cheater? No. Did I want to be honest for the first time in almost two months? Surprisingly, yes.

"I'm sorry," said Principal Davis, "but I find it impossible to believe that a straight-A, Stanford-bound student like you could be involved in something like this. Do you realize how extensive the operation was that Camden was running?"

"Six to ten workers at any given time, fifty to eighty clients both here and at Greenbrook, prices ranging from one hundred to five hundred dollars, depending on assignment, difficulty, deadline, subject, and grade guarantee," I said.

Principal Davis opened his mouth and shut it again.

"Camden handled the client side, and I handled the academic side," I continued. "We both handled the business aspects."

Silence.

"I mean, come on," I kept going. "Camden couldn't have done all the work himself. He couldn't have written those papers. He couldn't have done all those problem sets. He had to have help. The help was me." Oh, I was on a roll now. I sat up straighter, totally into it. "It started off as a pretty small operation, actually, and I never would have gotten involved in the first place except that I suddenly needed ten thousand dollars. Long story, you don't want to hear it, very boring. But anyway, yeah. It was us. The two of us. Both of us." I spit out the next sentence somewhat reluctantly, but I spit it out nonetheless. "He really shouldn't have to take all the blame."

Principal Davis sighed. "Maya, I'm not going to accept Camden King back into this school just because you ask me to."

"I'm not asking you to. I'm just telling you what I had to do with it."

"And I'm telling you that I'm satisfied that I've caught the culprit. He's got a bad track record, and it was really only a matter of time before he did something serious. But you—you're going to Stanford. Why are you trying to get yourself expelled too?"

"I'm not," I said. "I just want to do the right thing. However you choose to punish me, that's your decision." I mentally patted myself on the back for not having even the slightest waver in my voice when I said that, even though I knew that in that moment, I was probably kissing Stanford good-bye.

Principal Davis sighed deeply. "Well, if everything you just told me is true, I'll have no choice. Let's get your parents on the phone." He hit his intercom button. "Vivian? Can you put in a call to Maya Naravadee's parents, please?" There was a long pause. "Vivian?" he repeated. After a moment, Mrs. Hunter's voice came on.

"Yes, I can, but you might want to wait a minute because—" There was a hum of voices behind her and we couldn't hear her too well.

"What was that?" asked Principal Davis. "Can you repeat what you just said?"

"Yes, I said—" The hum behind her got louder, and there was a knock at the door. We started hearing voices coming through the door and over the intercom.

"If you'll all sit down and wait a moment—you can't just go in and—"

"There's no—"

"We just want to—"

"This is neither the time nor the—"

There was another knock at Principal Davis's office door, and before he had a chance to say anything, it opened. Mrs. Hunter, looking harried, stuck her head inside. Behind her, I could see Jonny, Cat, Bella, and a bunch of other kids. What the hell were they doing there? I knew they were mad at me, but were they so mad they wanted to show up and watch me get thrown out of school? How had they known I was here, anyway? I tried to make eye contact with Cat, but she was too busy whispering something urgently to Jonny; I tried to make eye contact with Bella, but she was too busy literally holding Darren back from barging into the office. Then I *did* make eye contact with someone, and I realized it was Sarah. Sarah?

"Hey," she mouthed at me. "Don't worry."

What the hell was—?

"What the hell is going on?" Principal Davis asked, beating me to it.

Mrs. Hunter, Jonny, Cat, Sarah, and everybody else crowded through the doorway and into the office. I looked around, bewildered—it was every person who'd ever done a fake assignment for the homework ring, including just the "work for hire" juniors, plus Dani. Had they all gotten in trouble? Had someone else ratted them out? And what was *Dani* doing here? Adding insult to injury by making out with Camden, and then following me around to mock me about it?

I'd gotten up from my chair, and Sarah stepped right up next to me. Principal Davis was standing now too, looking totally confused. Mrs. Hunter was in the doorway, also looking confused, plus guilty, and now, since two of her phone lines had started ringing, she looked frantic, too. She went to answer the phone.

"Principal Davis," Sarah started. Her voice was quiet as

usual, but full of resolve. "Just so you know, Camden King wasn't the only one behind the cheating ring. He was working with someone else, but it wasn't Maya. It was me."

"No," said Cat. "It was me."

"Actually, it was me," said Bella.

"It was me," said Darren.

"It was me," said Dani. Wait, what? What was she doing, trying to make up for stealing my boyfriend? I shot a glance at her, but she was too busy staring down her dad.

Nobody else said anything for a moment.

"I'm Spartacus," said Jonny.

Silence.

"I figured that would get a bigger laugh," he added. "Or one at all."

"I thought it was funny, just not laugh-out-loud funny," said Dani. "More of a dry humor, which is really your forte. So, good effort."

"Thank you, Dani. I appreciate that," said Jonny.

"You're welcome," she said. The room buzzed with a weird energy—it was tense, but for some reason, the tension didn't seem all that negative.

"*Ahem*," said Principal Davis. We all looked at him. "I was about to expel Maya for cheating," he said. "Are you saying you all want to be expelled as well?"

"She didn't do it," said Sarah.

"I *did* do it," I said. I felt a tiny glimmer of hope that

maybe the worst *wasn't* about to happen, but I still wasn't backing down from the truth.

"No, you didn't. I did," she said. She crossed her arms and didn't blink.

"Kids!" roared Principal Davis. "What is going on here? You all—you're all in the top five percent of your class! Well, most of you," he said, glancing at Dani. "I don't understand what's going on here. You're all smart kids, Ivy League–bound. Sarah, you're valedictorian! I just listened to Maya throw away her future, and you're all doing it as well?"

Nobody said anything. Nobody moved.

"Everybody out," said Principal Davis. "Out! Back to class. Go!"

"Okay, but, Daddy, are you gonna expel me? Because I'm not bothering to go back to class if you're gonna expel me," Dani said.

Principal Davis glared at her, then sighed. "Everybody just go sit in the waiting room," he snapped. He started shoving all of us out the door, where the three chairs by Mrs. Hunter's desk were quickly taken up by Darren and two of the random juniors. The rest of us sat on the floor. "No talking!" Principal Davis snapped. "Vivian, make sure they don't talk."

We all sat silently as Principal Davis disappeared back into his office and Mrs. Hunter shrugged at us apologetically. I was dying to ask someone—anyone—what was going on, but I had to settle for chewing my thumbnail down to a nub. After a few minutes, Vice Principal Rooker came through, stepping over our outstretched legs and backpacks that were strewn all over the floor. He went into the principal's office and we heard murmuring, punctuated by the occasional louder, but still incomprehensible, statement. After what seemed like forever, but was only sixteen minutes according to Mrs. Hunter's big, apple-shaped desk clock, Vice Principal Rooker flung open the door and waded through us again to leave. Principal Davis appeared in the doorway.

"All of you are suspended for three days," he said. "To be served at staggered intervals starting next week. Dani, you're also grounded for a month. I'm calling everyone's parents this afternoon. Now go back to class." He went back into his office and slammed the door.

Oh my God.

I wasn't expelled.

I was suspended—like everyone else—and I owed them all big-time. I still had no idea how any of this had just happened, and I had a dim realization that once all was said and done, this was probably still going to mess up things with Stanford . . . but I wasn't expelled.

A hand reached into my line of vision and I high-fived it without thinking. It was attached to Cat, who grinned at me as she picked up her backpack and headed out the door. What? How had she been furious at me a day ago and now suddenly—I couldn't finish my thought because Jonny reached toward me and did almost the same thing. He tugged a lock of my hair and grinned, and then picked up his stuff and went out the door. Dani went the opposite way—back into her dad's office, no doubt to protest being grounded along with the suspension—and as the door swung shut behind her, I turned to Sarah, who was now the only one left in the reception area with me.

"Uh . . ." I said hesitantly.

She grinned and tilted her head toward the door to the hallway, then stepped outside. "I'll explain everything."

I collected an excuse pass for first through fourth periods from Mrs. Hunter and then walked into the hallway and nudged Sarah on the shoulder with my own. "What the *hell* just happened?" I asked. "I mean, okay, I actually know what just happened, but—why? And why are *you* here? You didn't even have anything to do with *any* of it, and you agreed to come in here and confess to a fake crime?"

"What do you mean *agreed*?" Sarah asked innocently.

I stared at her. "Oh my God. This wasn't your idea, was it?"

She smiled and gave a tiny little curtsy. My jaw dropped open.

"You—you got everyone to come in here and—I mean—just to save my—? You could've gotten expelled along with me and Camden!" I exclaimed. "How did you—

how did you convince everyone to—" I bounced up and down on my tiptoes a little, nearly shaking with a mixture of glee and disbelief.

"Please, like Davis was ever gonna take down the average G.P.A. of this school that much. He'd lose all his extra funding," Sarah scoffed. "Everybody knew that . . . at least, once I pointed it out, everybody knew that. And the people who needed extra convincing, well, I may have casually threatened to turn them in." She smiled mischievously. "Don't give me that much credit. It wasn't *that* risky."

"It totally was," I said. "It *totally* was."

"Yeah, well, it was worth it," she said. "Believe me, I'm collecting on this one. Forever."

"Oh my God, please do," I said. "But I still can't believe everyone would—I mean, don't they think that I'm just a horrible person who—"

"No, they don't," Sarah said. "I told them about the fine. And about Leonard, that vile little punk. I figured when you weren't in class this morning that the guilt had probably gotten to you, and then I saw that note you left me, and I *knew* it had." She looked at me and I gave her a sheepish grin, which she returned. "And I figured right. And so I figured I'd do something about it."

I contemplated this as the lunch bell rang and kids started filtering into the hallway around us. I dropped everything I was holding onto the floor and threw my arms around Sarah as tightly as I could. She squeaked in surprise, sounding like she couldn't breathe, but I wouldn't let go. "Thank you!" I cried. "And bless you for not holding a grudge! I am so, so sorry I said all those terrible things to you that day in the tutoring office!"

"Oh, yes! Make out!" some guy yelled from down the hall. I flipped off whoever it was without looking, as Sarah laughed and disentangled herself from me. Then I dragged us into the girls' bathroom so that we wouldn't be subject to any more Girls Gone Wild–type suggestions from passing randoms.

"Oh my God!" she said, lightly shoving me. "*I'm* sorry! I *was* jealous, you called it, and I was acting like a total six-year-old about it!"

"No," I insisted. "It was all my fault. Hello, look how wrong I turned out to be about Camden. And look how right *you* were. He turned out to be such a sketch—" I couldn't finish the sentence. An unpleasant shiver had gone down my spine as I thought, yet again, about what had happened with Camden Saturday night.

"Yeah, about that," said a voice. Sarah and I both turned around.

Dani had just come in.

"Oh, hi," I said flatly, stepping away from her. I wasn't looking where I was going, the result being that my back slammed into one of the wall-mounted hand dryers. The impact caused a sharp pain to my spine, while also seeming to liberate a word from my mouth that I don't *think* I meant to say: "Slut."

Dani laughed and crossed over to the wall mirror to start putting on mascara. "Seriously?" she asked, running a hand over her already smooth hair. "Slut? That's not even creative."

"Creative, no. Truth, yes," I said, standing my ground. A few months ago, I probably would have ducked out of her way. Who am I kidding, a few months ago I never would have spoken to her in the first place, much less called her a ho. But hey, it had been a month and a half of firsts for me, including the first time I'd ever walked in on my boyfriend making out with some other girl—so why the heck not? "I mean, thanks for doing what you did just now in your dad's office, I appreciate that," I said. "What I *don't* appreciate is—"

Dani cut me off. "Maya. Honey," she said, taking a black eye pencil out of her purse and fearlessly lining her inner rims with it. "You're supposed to be the smart one, and you haven't figured it out yet?"

"Figured what out?" I asked warily. I looked over at Sarah, who shrugged.

"Why Camden didn't rat you out when my dad hauled him out of class yesterday?"

Next to me, I felt Sarah tense up. "Okay, why?" I asked Dani cautiously.

"My dad was onto you guys last week," she said, turning away from the mirror to look at me. "I warned Cam that something might go down soon, and he asked me to help him piss you off enough that you'd let him take the fall alone if something happened. The whole thing with your friends finding out about you guys taking a percentage, well, he didn't plan on that. But people start talking when they start drinking."

I stared at her.

"Yeah, the party didn't exactly get more fun after you flipped out and ran away," she added. "But, like I said, the hot tub thing was a setup."

I gripped the edge of one of the sinks to keep from falling over. It was wet, which was disgusting, but I held on anyway, as my head got dizzy and my stomach did backflips. If you ever wanted to know what hope, plus dread, plus Tootsie Pop tastes like coming back up, the answer is sour Gummi worms. Gross, but true.

"Wait. So . . ." I was still struggling to stand, and now I was struggling to talk. "So . . . so you and he weren't really . . ."

"Please," Dani said coolly. "Like I would ever voluntarily hook up with Cam? The guy's like my freakin' brother. Sophomore year was just some sort of weird experiment." She chucked her array of eye makeup back into her purse and paused in the doorway on her way out. "The point of all this is that he really likes you. In fact, I've totally never seen him like this over a girl before. So give him a second chance, for chrissakes. And call me later. We should all go shopping again sometime soon—I need new shoes." She glanced down at my feet, which were clad in some of my brother's ratty old childhood sneakers. "So do you," she added teasingly.

Then she grinned at me, waved at Sarah, and left.

I tried to breathe again.

Oh, God.

Camden had sacrificed himself. He'd taken all the blame so that I wouldn't get in trouble. He'd hidden the truth so that I wouldn't get hurt. Christ, he'd gone on a suicide mission and taken himself down . . . and he'd done it all for me.

My phone rang.

It was him.

My eyes widened, and I wordlessly showed the phone to Sarah.

"Answer it," she said, smiling. "I'll see you in class." She pushed open the bathroom door and walked off, as I leaned back against the wall and looked at my ringing phone again. *Camden*, it blinked at me. *Camden. Camden.*

I took a deep breath and answered it.

chapter twenty

"So, what're you gonna do with your three-day vacation?"
Camden asked. It was a few days later. We were up in the
woods behind the school; the afternoon was warm and
sunny, and it had been long enough so that it was possible
to sit on a stump, which was what I was doing, or lean back
against a tree, which was what Camden was doing, without
getting wet from the drizzle that had been coming down
earlier that morning. We were both in jeans and T-shirts
(mine was cropped—a nod to Dani's fashion sense), and I
was wearing flip-flops for the first time that spring, the better to show off the sparkly blue pedicure I'd given myself.

"My three-day *suspension*," I said, throwing my head
back and my arms out in order to stretch my face toward
the sunshine, "will be spent catching up on all my own
homework that I've been skimping on for the past month,
and getting used to the idea of being stuck in Michigan

forever. Or at least for another four years." After what Sarah had done for me, I couldn't stomach the the possibility that she'd get any trouble from Stanford about the suspensions we'd all gotten, so I'd written them a letter telling them what had happened, in order to make sure that her record remained spotless. Unfortunately . . .

"So Stanford's really not letting you in, huh?" Camden asked.

"Oh, they are," I said. "It's the scholarship that's the problem. I think all those über-rich donors are pretty confident that they can find another kid with my grades and test scores who needs the money more, and by 'needs the money more' I mean 'didn't mastermind an elaborate multi-thousand-dollar cheating ring.' So now we can't really afford anything but in-state."

"I gotta give you credit," Camden said. "You don't even sound that bummed."

"Whatever, I got what I deserved." I shrugged, feeling a tinge of remorse flutter up but then quickly settle down again. I'd spent the previous day in a stupor over the fact that my Stanford dream was dead—and by my own hand— but now all my panic had resolved itself into a sort of quiet, calm acceptance. Going to University of Michigan wasn't exactly a tragedy—it might have been my safety school, but it was a kickass one nonetheless. "Anyway," I added, "I'll just go to Stanford for med school."

Camden raised an eyebrow at me. "Little overconfident there, don't you think?" he asked, nudging me with his foot.

I kicked back at him playfully. "I learned from the master," I said. He grinned and stepped over to where I was sitting, lowering himself to the ground next to me and leaning his head on my knee.

"Well, at least you aren't gonna be three thousand miles away next year," he said.

"Not from here," I agreed. "But maybe from you—you don't know where you're gonna end up yet," I pointed out, running my hand gently through his hair as he looked up at me. His waves were already a bit lighter now from the sun than they'd been a few months ago during the dark of winter.

"Probably nowhere," he said cheerfully. "I can't believe my parents actually cracked down this hard. I mean, military school? Am I gonna get raped?"

"That's prison," I said.

"Same difference. I'll be away from you," he said.

My heart went, *Awww!* My hand kept ruffling his hair. My mouth couldn't think of anything good to say, but it didn't seem to matter; his arm snaked around my lower legs and hugged them to himself.

"Anyway," he continued, "you can come visit. It's only like, a two-hour drive."

"Three," I said.

"Two and a half if you speed," he said. "Plus, if I actually get hard-core about grades and stuff, maybe I can go to Michigan next year too."

I took his head in my hands and twisted it up so that he could see the look I was giving him.

"Okay, okay, Michigan State," he said, grinning.

I smiled and kissed his forehead. "All right, so what do you think? Time to go?"

"I dunno," said Camden. "What do you think, Leonard?" he called.

We both looked over at a large tree about fifteen feet away. From behind it peeked Leonard, wearing just his shoes, socks, and some exceedingly lame boxers with those fake lipstick marks all over them.

"Can you believe he fell for that text you sent him?" Camden asked me, purposefully loud enough for Leonard to hear.

"I'm hot. Who wouldn't fall for it?" I asked innocently.

"Wow," said Camden, "you really did learn from me, didn't you?"

I smiled sweetly, then turned to look at Leonard, who had approached us and was shivering despite the sun.

"Come on, you guys," he said, his voice sounding as desperate as I'm sure mine had the day he blackmailed me. "Can I have my clothes back?"

"I dunno. Can we have our five grand back?" asked Camden, standing up.

"I already spent it!"

"Then no," I said. I picked up my backpack and swung it over my shoulder as Camden put his arm around me, and we started back toward the parking lot.

"You can't leave me here!" Leonard yelled after us. "What if it starts to rain again? I'm gonna freeze to death! I'm gonna catch pneumonia! I'm gonna sue you guys!"

We ignored him.

Back at the car, Camden clicked it unlocked and then opened the passenger-side door for me. I got in and waited for him to come around the other side and slide behind the wheel. He started to turn the key, but I put my hand on his arm and stopped him. There was something that had been bugging me that we hadn't talked about yet.

"Okay," I said. "I have to know." He turned to look at me and I kept going. "Why did you do it? Why did you like, orchestrate something so elaborate and risky just so that I wouldn't get in trouble? Why'd you want to take the fall alone?"

He gazed at me steadily. "Because I'm in love with you."

Oh. Good answer.

Camden leaned forward, brushed my hair out of my

eyes, and kissed me . . . and if either of us had been paying attention, we would've heard chaos outside the windows as Leonard sprinted past the car in his underwear and everyone in the parking lot laughed hysterically.

But we weren't paying attention.

acknowledgments

Many thanks to Josh Bank, Allison Heiny, Bob Levy, Les Morgenstein, Katie McConnaughey, Sara Shandler, Andrea C. Uva, Siobhan Vivian, Farrin Jacobs, Lexa Hillyer, everyone at Alloy Entertainment and HarperTeen, David Boxerbaum, and Helena Heyman.

Ever wish there were two of you?
Well, be careful what you wish for . . .

★

Read on for a sneak peek of
Cherry Cheva's latest novel,

DUPLIKATE.

Fwamp. Fwamp. Fwamp. I tried to slam the snooze button on my alarm clock and realized that both of my arms were completely tangled in the blankets. Great. I wiggled around to free myself and finally turned off the alarm. Snuggling back under the covers, I was getting back to that blissful early morning half-sleep when I heard a voice.

"Don't you think you should just get up?"

"What? No," I said, not bothering to open my eyes. "There's a snooze button for a reason." I was halfway asleep again when I realized that the voice did not belong to my mother.

I'm not gonna lie—I shrieked bloody murder. Then I scooched backward across my bed as fast as I could and scrunched up against the wall, my body in an upright fetal position, my heels on one of my pillows. I held another pillow in front of me, like that would save me, and struggled to keep myself from breathing either way too hard or not at all.

But the stranger in my room clearly wasn't a murderer. She was a teenage girl. About five six, wavy dark brown hair falling just past her shoulders, brown eyes, a decent complexion—not perfect, but pretty good. Couple freckles on the cheekbones. She was smiling and she wasn't holding a gun or a knife. All in all, if there was going to be a random stranger in your room, this was not a bad person for her to look like.

Except that she looked exactly like me.

"Mom!" I screeched.

"She left for work already," the NotMe said. "Hi!"

"Hi?" I replied, looking around my room frantically. Everything looked the same as usual: piles of books on the floor, clothes draped on every surface, random pens and pencils scattered on my desk and dresser, the edge of my computer monitor covered in Post-it notes. The door to my walk-in closet was open, which was weird because I closed it at night, and the overhead light was on even though I hadn't yet left my bed, but mostly everything looked normal.

Except for the girl. Who looked like me.

"I'm hallucinating," I said out loud. "This is why one

should always say no to drugs."

"Who the hell are you?" I demanded. I was still backed up against the wall, and the girl was now coming toward me. She settled happily at the foot of my bed, sitting cross-legged and hugging one of my pillows. "Don't touch my stuff," I added. She put the pillow down.

"What, seriously? You don't know?" she asked. "I'm Rina!"

I stared at her blankly.

"Rina," she repeated. Another blank stare from me. "Nice to meet you," she continued. "Or me, I guess." She giggled.

"You're not me," I said. Except that she kind of was. Actually, she totally was, except for the fact that instead of flannel jammie pants and a T-shirt, she had on a fuzzy pink tracksuit and a ton of lip gloss. And body glitter. Her cheekbones and the backs of her hands were completely covered in body glitter. Ew, tacky. What was going on here?

When in doubt and fearing for your own sanity, be rude. "What kind of a freak name is Rina?" I demanded.

"Um, the freak name you gave me 'cause you thought it was a cooler nickname for Katerina than Kate," she said. "Hello! You signed on last night! Finally! It's been forever!" She pointed happily at my computer. I looked too. It was still frozen, the "Welcome to SimuLife!" window stuck open.

Oh no. Wait. The wheels turned in my head . . . Simu-Life . . . what kind of a game was SimuLife, and what did it have to do with this girl in my—oh. Uh oh.

Duh.

She was the version of me from the game. That made no sense, but it sort of made sense. Leave it to my hallucination to sort of make sense. "So . . . you're my SimuLife self?" I asked shakily, blinking a few times in a mixture of confusion and horror.

"Yeah!" Rina nodded happily. "I knew we were smart! Thanks for busting me out. The last time we saw each other was what, eighth grade? It's been a while."

We stared at each other for a moment, then my alarm clock went off again. Thanks, snooze button. But the repetitive blare gave me a sudden moment of clarity. I jumped off my bed, walked over to my computer, and yanked out the power cord. Good-bye, SimuLife! Good-bye, weird girl in my room!

I turned around. Rina was still there.